SUMMER BUCKET LIST

SUMMER BUCKET LIST

a novel by T.K. Rapp

Summer Bucket List
by T.K. Rapp

Cover Design by T.K. Rapp
Edited by Amy Jackson
Cover Images Courtesy ~ AndrewLozovyl, Vadymvdrobot, Wavebreakmedia, AllaSerebrina/Depositphotos
Copyright © 2019 T.K. Rapp
All rights reserved.

ISBN-13: 9781098512170

Dedication

To my Grams
Though your memories may fade, I will carry your stories in my
heart. Always.

CHAPTER 1

HOLLAND

"Senior class, please rise," Emilia Santiago, the class president, announced to the cheers and applause of everyone in the stands.

I did as instructed, glancing into the crowd at my mom and dad, whose smiles could be seen a mile away. I was the last of the Monroe clan, the third kid, to finish high school. Come August their nest would be empty, and if I thought about it too much, I might cry. Instead, I turned to my left and smiled at Jeffery Morris, the guy who'd always been next to me for school functions——and this would be the last.

"Graduates, with your left hand, move your tassel to the left," Emilia continued.

All four hundred of us made the symbolic move and waited for the official announcement.

Emilia stepped backward as Mr. Percival, the principal, approached the podium and cleared his throat.

"Ladies and gentlemen, it's my pleasure to present to you the graduating class of 2019."

It took only seconds for the sea of blue caps to be tossed into the air, mine included. A surge of pure exhilaration ran through me because I was finally done. While there were shouts and whistling from the stands, with my classmates it was hugs and smiles. My best friend, Megan, who was a few rows ahead of mine, turned around to find me and smiled.

"We did it!" she shouted as everyone around us continued to cheer.

I didn't expect to be so emotional, but there I was, tears running down my face as the culmination of twelve years of hard work came to an end, the next chapter of my life only beginning. She walked toward me, greeting friends along the way until she reached me.

"Are you crying?" she asked, pulling me into a hug.

"No," I lied with a laugh, returning the hug.

The chairs that we had sat in for the last two hours were scattered about the coliseum floor as all of our classmates found their friends. It probably looked like pure chaos, but no one cared.

"Holland," I heard a familiar voice call out.

I turned to see Colin walking toward me.

He carried his blue cap in his hand, dodging people who were trying to find one another. My handsome friend, who I had known since I was three, reached us but stopped short and threw his arms up in the air. "We did it!"

"Congratulations," I said, hugging him tightly.

"You, too." He kissed the top of my head, like he always did, and then turned to Megan to hug her.

"We need a picture," I said, pulling out my phone to take a selfie.

Meg and Colin stood on either side of me and we took several funny ones and one of us making sad faces. But my favorite was the one of them kissing my cheeks. Those two had been by my side for every major event. Through breakups, failed tests, fights with my sister, my acceptance into college, and everything in between, they were my people.

"Okay, so what now?" Colin asked as I finished taking some of him and Meg together.

"I promised Mom and Dad we'd get something to eat after this was over. What about you two?" I asked.

"Same," Meg said. "We're still meeting up later?"

"Sounds good," I answered before turning to Colin. "Want to come eat?"

"I would, but I told Chris we could do something before heading to Knox's party. Are you still going?" he asked.

"Yep. We'll be there later."

"Okay, then I'll see you later."

He kissed both of our cheeks before taking off to find Chris and the others. Megan and I would see each other after our respective dinners, so we hugged once more before walking off to find our parents. My classmates were still congratulating each other as I passed, a few of them stopping me along the way.

I didn't expect to miss them, but as I said goodbye, I knew I would. I would miss walking the halls and talking to my friends. I would miss seeing Colin and Meg every day—they were my best friends in the world, and both would be leaving for college across the country. I would miss all of it.

And then I saw Blake.

My ex. I could confidently admit that I would not miss him. Not even for a second.

I briefly looked around to see if there was another path I could take, but unfortunately, it was not promising. To get to my family I would have to pass by the jerk I had wasted five months on. Luckily, he was talking to his best friend and new girlfriend, so maybe he would stay distracted long enough for me to pass.

"Damn it," I groaned under my breath, dipping my head so we wouldn't make eye contact. As I started to walk, my arm brushed against someone else, but before I could speak, he did.

"Excuse me?" the low voice said.

"I'm sorry," I said absently as I turned to see who I had run into, only to see Milo Davis' dark brown eyes boring into me, his typical brooding scowl in place.

I sighed, ready for the usual banter we'd always shared. I had never had a problem with Milo, and I didn't think he had a problem with me, but he had always alternated between sarcastic and annoyed when it came to me. I never could tell if he was giving me a hard time or if he just hated me.

Milo was tall, with dark brown hair and a smile that, when it was the right smile, would cause a dimple would appear. There were times I found myself staring at the small scar beneath his eyebrow, the one that made him look slightly dangerous. I always wished I knew the story behind the scar, but since it was a mystery, I had imagined it was from dirt biking or some other daredevil event. Since we never really talked about anything other than school, there was little I knew about him and I was left to create a profile that I liked. He was attractive in that artsy, "I don't give a damn" sort of way. Not that Milo was actually artsy at all. I had worked with him on enough projects to know that engineering was what he liked.

Standing in front of me, he had his usually messy hair brushed out of his eyes, and I was mesmerized because I could see him...and how handsome he looked.

"Not you. Sorry," I stammered.

"Of course not," he muttered before rolling his eyes and turning his back to me.

For four years we had shared annoyed glares directed at each other and our classmates. I heard the scoffs and grunts whenever I spoke, and the snide remarks that he thought no one else heard.

But I was aware of them all. And each time, I pretended not to notice.

Before I thought better of it, I reached out my hand, placed it on his arm, and gave a gentle tug so he would face me. As he turned toward me, he looked at where my hand touched his

4

arm and then his eyes met mine.

"Milo, not sure if I ever did anything to make you dislike me…"

He opened his mouth to speak, but I kept talking.

"…but I just wanted to tell you congratulations and wish you luck."

I dropped my hand from his arm and took a step away as I flashed a smile. I would miss the sarcastic banter we had engaged in, and I had always hoped that maybe we would be friends, but it had never come to pass.

As I walked backward, Milo disappearing in the crowd, I had started to slowly turn around when I caught the hint of a lopsided smile from him. It felt like a small triumph that came too late, but I still counted it as a win. I turned around, weirdly pleased that a smile could make me feel so good, forgetting that my whole mission was to avoid Blake.

"Hey, Holland," Blake said when I ran right into his toned, football-playing chest.

I swallowed hard and took a step back, looking at him and his girlfriend Sammi.

"Um, hey," I managed to say as my heart thudded in my chest.

We had broken up a month earlier, and while I was still single, he had managed to pick up his new girlfriend within days of the breakup. Since I was in all honors classes and he…wasn't…I rarely saw him and had been able to successfully avoid him when the chance arose. I knew the day would come when I would have to face him, and it was time to rip off the Band-Aid.

"Congratulations on the scholarship," I said. "Full ride?"

"Nah, just the first year. We'll see how that goes."

"Well, good luck," I said, and then turned to Sammi. "You, too."

"Thanks. I—" she started to say when I interrupted her.

"Sorry, my mom is right over there looking for me." I looked at Blake one last time and smiled——my own silent goodbye to the guy I once thought I loved. "Good luck."

Before he could respond, I made my way over to my mom, who could not seem to stop smiling. Her eyes were red with unshed tears, but I knew she was saving those for August when I moved two hundred miles away for college.

"Baby girl! I'm so proud of you," she gushed when I was finally in front of her.

"Thanks, Mom," I said, looking around for the rest of the family.

"They're already at the restaurant. Dad told them to meet us there."

"And where's Dad?"

"Right here, honey," he said, handing me a bouquet of flowers. "Congratulations, Holland. We're so proud of you."

"Thanks, Daddy."

"Did I see you and Blake talking?" he asked.

Mom elbowed his stomach and he looked from her to me, confused at his obvious gaffe.

"It's okay, Mom. Yes, I accidentally ran into him, so I had to make small talk."

"How was that?"

"Awkward. But at least I don't have to see him again," I answered, thankful that it was the truth.

"Who was that other boy I saw you talking to?" Mom asked.

I turned around and looked down at the crowd that had begun to scatter and spotted Milo talking with two other people. I found myself staring a little longer than I should, but he was smiling and enjoying himself. Milo rarely smiled. If he did, I was certain more girls would have taken notice of him, because it lit up his whole face.

"Holland?" she asked, snapping me back into the

conversation.

"That was Milo."

"The same Milo you were always griping about?" she asked.

"Yep. Just wished him luck. That was it."

"Well, that was sweet of you."

"Trust me, it went in one ear and out the other," I scoffed.

"I don't think so," Mom said. "I mean, I watched after you walked away, and he didn't stop staring at you."

"He didn't?" I asked.

Mom smiled at me and Dad looked at the floor as if trying to locate the subject of our current conversation.

"What does that mean?" Dad questioned, looking between Mom and me.

"Nothing," I said. "Nothing at all."

I looked back down at the remaining crowd, unable to find Milo. I had gotten a smile, but I was certain Mom was imagining the prolonged stare. I had always been pretty certain that when it came to me, Milo was not a fan.

"Come on," Mom said. "Let's go meet up with everyone."

I looked back one last time and noticed Milo across the room near an exit. He stood alone, and it almost seemed as though he was looking at me. Maybe even smiling.

But two smiles in one day was unheard of. Three, impossible.

***

"To Holland," Dad announced, lifting up his glass of water, everyone else following suit.

"Dad," I groaned, hating the attention.

"What?" he laughed. "You're the last Monroe to graduate. Before long, you'll be out of the house and making decisions on your own."

"Hasn't she always done that?" Mom teased. "Remember

when she was five and she walked into the living room when we were watching TV? She stood in front of us and said that from now on, she would no longer eat meat. She was so cute, I almost didn't have the heart to tell her that hot dogs were made of meat."

"But you did," I laughed. "And then I cried because I didn't want to give up hot dogs."

"Yeah, that lasted all of five minutes." Ben, my older brother grinned. "But what about the time she wanted to stay up all night and watch TV?"

"I remember that," Marcie gasped before laughing. "Mom said that it was okay."

"I thought for sure she'd fall asleep watching a movie," Mom said, shaking her head.

"But I didn't."

"And Mom was pissed," Marcie added, and then did her best Mom impersonation. "Holland Nicole Monroe! Don't you ever stay up late like that again. Do you hear me?"

Mom burst into giggles at Marcie's impression as she tried to deny it, but we all knew it to be true.

"I was seven," I said. "I was just trying to see if I could do it."

"And clearly you could," Dad said. "See, this is what I'm talking about. With all three of you gone, what are your mother and I going to have around to entertain us?"

"You and Mom are like the perfect couple," I said sweetly. "I'm sure the two of you will be just fine."

"Well, we've all had to hear how empty the house is when we leave. Now it's your turn," Marcie said as she gave me her most sympathetic look.

"Dad, cut her a break," Ben interjected. "Holland can't handle that guilt like Marse and me."

"Yeah, listen to him," I said, patting my brother's back. "Ben knows how fragile I am."

His fiancée Harper laughed and leaned her head on Ben's shoulder. She was the first girlfriend that he had brought around that we all liked, so when he had decided to propose, we were thrilled.

"What's the plan for the summer?" Harper asked.

"Getting things packed. Work. The usual."

"Holland," she said, shaking her head. "You're the most responsible eighteen-year-old I know. Maybe you could just relax and enjoy your last summer before you start being an adult."

"No rest for the wicked," Marcie said with a laugh. "Besides, I've never known Holland to just sit still. Ever."

"I did decide to work at the country club. Tips are better, the hours aren't too bad, and I can use the pool on my off days."

"When did you decide this?" Mom asked, as well as the rest of the eyes that were on me. "And why am I just hearing about it now?"

"I dropped off an application yesterday and they called me this morning before the ceremony. They want me to start tomorrow."

"Wow. But you loved working at Grady's," Marcie said.

"It's not a big deal. I can always go back to the diner if I want. Ms. Meadows is always looking for help. But the hours and tips are better at the club."

"It's sort of the end of an era," Marcie said. "You've been working there since you were sixteen."

"I know."

"Are you sure this is what you want?" she asked, her mothering tone beginning to surface.

My sister was two years older than me, but always thought of me as a child. Sometimes I wanted to yell at her to stop treating me like a kid, but for the most part I just let it go.

"Yes. Now, can we change the subject?" I asked, taking a sip of my drink.

Luckily, there was no need to make a big deal about anything because the food came out just in time to be the perfect distraction. The waitstaff set the food in front of us, and the first minute that followed was spent in wonderful silence, each of us enjoying our meal.

"What time are you and Megan getting together?" Dad asked.

"Seven," I answered after swallowing a mouthful of food. "I'm staying at her house, if that's okay."

"Fine with me. Just be sure to text us when you get home," Dad said.

Marcie opened her mouth to object, but she was silenced with a glare from Mom. I looked at my sister and smirked, because I knew she was about to bring up the fact that she had not been allowed to do anything on her graduation night. Granted, she had spent the night before drinking so much that she had bloodshot eyes in her graduation photos. Mom and Dad were pissed about that one.

"I'll do one better and text you from the party to let you know we made it," I said, ever the annoying sister that Marcie deemed me to be.

CHAPTER 2

HOLLAND

Mr. Clarke held the door open as I walked in, and gave me a warm hug. The Clarkes were like my second family, and they were always expecting my arrival. I did not get to see them at the graduation ceremony because they had their own plans with Meg. There was never a time that felt anything other than loved in the Clarke home.

"We're so proud of you," Mr. Clarke said.

"Is that Holland?" Mrs. Clarke asked from the kitchen.

"Now who else would it be?" I teased.

She walked into the living room wearing her biggest smile as she pulled me into her arms. Her hugs always relaxed me; it was like she had some magical power that had the ability to make me feel calm.

"We have a little something for you," she said as she loosened her embrace. "Honey, can you get the bag off the counter?"

Mr. Clarke disappeared for a moment and returned with a

small gift bag with silver tissue paper sticking out from the top. He wrapped his arm around his wife and they smiled while they waited for me to open the bag. When I finally did, inside I found a silver keychain with a picture of Meg and me when we were little girls. I smiled as I studied the image, vividly remembering our trip to the zoo. I looked at Meg's parents and grinned.

"Turn it over," Mrs. Clarke said, smiling eagerly.

When I did, I saw a picture of the two of us from a month earlier. Our faces were smooshed together as we hugged tightly, the biggest grins on our faces.

"You two are the best," I said, pulling them both to me as I hugged them.

"It's nothing big, but we thought you two would like to have something to keep with you, even when you can't be together. We gave Meg hers earlier."

"I love it. Thank you."

"Holland? Is that you?" Meg shouted from her room.

"Yeah!" I called out.

"C'mon up."

"Be right there."

"How was your dinner?" Mrs. Clarke asked.

"Great," I answered. "I went home and even took a little nap."

Mr. Clarke laughed and shook his head. "Something tells me you two are going to be late getting home."

"We'll be quiet," I said over my shoulder as I walked to Meg's room.

"Do you really think we won't hear?" he laughed.

"Go on up," Mrs. Clarke said, playfully swatting at her husband's shoulder.

I walked up to Meg's room and found her sitting in front of her vanity fixing her hair. She was wearing a new shirt that we had bought the weekend before and her favorite ripped jeans.

She was never one to wear much makeup, so I was surprised to see her completely made up, and her dark blond hair styled with tousled waves.

"Damn, Meg. Who are you going to see tonight?" I teased. "You look hot."

"Thanks." She blushed. "And no one."

She stood up from her seat and walked to the jewelry box on her dresser. She was rifling through the pieces until she found the necklace she was looking for.

"Can you help me with this?" she asked, handing the gold chain and medal to me.

"I haven't seen you wear this in forever. I thought you lost it."

"Me too," she laughed. "Guess where it was?"

"In your car?" I teased.

Her four-door sedan was the place trash, books, and small things went to die. Honestly, for all the grief I gave her about how messy it was, she rarely bothered to clean it.

"No," she shot back quickly with a playful scowl. "In my leather jacket. The one my parents got me last year."

"No way. I guess that just shows you don't wear it nearly enough."

"I know. I was packing one of my boxes up and the necklace fell out when I put the jacket in there."

A wave of sadness washed over me at the mention of packing. While I had another three months before I had to move, Megan was leaving in a week. She had signed up to take summer courses at Stedham Tech, so she had to leave sooner. A whole summer without my best friend would be miserable enough, but for the next four years we would be a thousand miles apart.

I feared what it meant for our friendship, but I refused to let that thought derail the one good week that we did have together.

"I know that look," Meg said as she walked toward me.

"Nope. I'm good," I lied, fixing my most convincing smile on my face. "Just had a moment and I'm totally fine now."

She cocked her head to the side and waited for some indication that I was lying. If she saw it, she chose to ignore it and went back to getting ready.

"That dress looks great on you," she said.

I had bought a beige T-shirt dress that hugged me in the right places. Paired with my white Converse, it was a casual and comfortable outfit. Usually I was the one to get dressed up while Megan went for laid back, but it was evident we had switched for the night.

She walked over and handed me a hair tie because, no matter how short my hair was, I always had it pulled up into a ponytail. At the current uneven shoulder length, it made for a cute tiny nub of a ponytail.

"No thanks," I said, messing my hair up a little.

"What? No ponytail?" she gasped mockingly. "Just kidding. I love it down."

"Figured I wore it down for the ceremony, why put it up now," I said with a shrug.

I sat on her bed while I waited for her to finish getting ready, and started scrolling through Instagram. Friends had posted their graduation pictures and I smiled, knowing I had done the same.

"So," Meg said as she put the final touches on her face. "Did I see you talking to Milo?"

"Did you?" I asked, ignoring her insinuating tone as I continued to scroll through my screen.

"He looked…intense."

"He's always intense," I answered. "Besides, it was the lesser of two evils. I was avoiding one, and bumped into the other."

"Other?"

"Yeah, I was trying to avoid Blake and Sammi and ended up running into Milo. Literally. He's always such an ass to me, and I don't know why."

"It's just his personality. He's really a nice guy."

"See, I thought so too, but he always blew me off, no matter how nice I was to him."

"I wouldn't be too hard on the guy. I think he's had some personal things going on," Meg said.

"That's fine, but it doesn't mean you have to be a jerk."

"True. But just remember, you never know what's going on in someone else's life."

"I know you're right…it's just, well…never mind."

"No way, you don't get to do that," she said, putting her lipstick in her pocket as she walked toward me. Meg grabbed her phone and her purse and stood in front of me with her arms crossed. "You know the rules."

I rolled my eyes and stood up, reminding her that I was a good two inches taller than her five-foot-five frame. She raised a brow, her stance unmoving, and I exhaled loudly.

"I hate the rules," I grumbled.

"So…"

"Well, after I talked to him, which couldn't even be considered a conversation, I went to talk to my mom. She said that he watched me walk away…with a smile on his face."

Megan gasped in horror and then laughed. "Heaven forbid Milo smile. What's wrong with that?"

"Nothing, I guess. It's just not something he ever did with me. He always seemed so distant, avoiding any conversation at all. But then I thought I saw him looking at me before I left the graduation."

"Hollz, I've always thought he had a thing for you," she said.

"What?" I asked, feeling my stomach drop at her words. "Milo Davis?"

"Yeah. I mean, I know he's not big on talking to everyone, but he's really nice."

"How do you know so much about him?"

"I don't...not really, anyway. I've just seen him around town. When he's not at school, he's a completely different person."

"Okay, now I know you're crazy. I saw him at the movies just a few weeks ago and he avoided me like the plague."

"Yeah, well most guys avoided you because of Blake, so there's always that."

"My head hurts, I can't talk about this anymore. Are you ready to go?"

"I'm ready when you are, but you realize we're going to be the first people at Knox's if we go now," she reminded me.

"Honestly, it's fine."

"All right, then let's go."

***

We knocked on the door and were greeted by the tall, handsome, muscular Knox—co-captain of the football team. He and I had been friends since sophomore year, when he had needed help in Spanish class. Once I started dating Blake, our friendship had become a bit strained because of Blake's jealous streak, but we had managed to stay somewhat close.

"Hey, Holland," Knox said as he answered the door, a beer in hand. He pulled me into a hug, lifting me off the ground before setting me to my feet again.

"Sorry we're so early," I said.

"No worries." He grinned. "Hey, Meg. How's it going?"

Though Meg and I were always together, she was usually quiet in a party setting. It always took her a long time to warm up to other people, including Knox. He was one of the nicest guys I knew—always inclusive of others, including Meg.

When she didn't answer his questions, I gave her a discrete nudge and she shook her head and smiled.

"Sorry. I'm good."

In a very uncharacteristically Meg move, she stepped forward and wrapped her arms around his neck and gave him a hug. Knox's eyes were wide, no doubt thinking the same thing as him. I'd never seen Megan Clarke actually flirt with anyone; she always said she was too shy. But what I saw was most definitely Meg flirting.

"Glad you could make it."

"Thanks for inviting us." Her voice was almost singsong.

"Can I get you two a drink?" he asked.

"I'm on duty tonight," I said, pointing at Megan, and he nodded.

"Thanks for that," he said.

"I'll take a beer," Megan said as we followed Knox into the kitchen.

A few friends were there talking when we walked into the room. We said our hellos and chatted about the ceremony, but conversation stopped half an hour later when Blake made his entrance. Sammi started holding his hand and smiling up at him as soon as she spotted me. I didn't have a problem with Sammi—not really, anyway. She was dating my ex; that was it.

"Wow, twice in one day," Blake said with a smirk as he looked at me before turning his attention to the host. "Hey, Knox. How's it going?"

"It's going," Knox said.

I watched as he turned his back to Blake, resuming his conversation with Meg and the others.

It was odd to me because Knox and Blake had played football together for years. When Blake and I would go to parties, we always hung out with the guys. But from the looks of it, the guys were sort of phasing Blake out. Not that I minded. It made me feel a bit more at ease that I wasn't being excluded.

"What are we talking about?" Blake asked, trying to get in on the conversation.

"Meg's telling us about her classes."

"Oh yeah…so when do you leave?" Knox asked Megan.

"In a week."

"Wow. A week?" Blake turned his attention to me and raised his chin. "What are you going to do without your shadow, Hollz?"

At that, I felt my skin grow hot, rage boiling beneath the surface. Meg was not, and had never been, my shadow. She certainly was not someone that just hid behind the scenes. She was my best friend, and he was making light of how much we would miss each other. Before I could open my mouth, I noticed Knox look down at Meg, who seemed as disappointed as me. He wrapped an arm around her shoulder and hugged her against him. I had never been more proud to call Knox a friend than I was at that moment.

"Meg? A shadow? You must be thinking of someone else."

Blake had the decency to look remorseful and opened his mouth to speak, but Knox reached out for Meg's hand. "There's some people out back. Wanna come with me?"

She nodded and allowed Knox to hold her hand as he guided her outside. When I was sure she was out of earshot, I turned to Blake, who shifted uncomfortably where he stood.

"Why are you such a jerk to her? She's never been anything but nice to you."

"Aw c'mon, Holland. I didn't mean anything by it."

"It was just a joke," Sammi added.

I looked from Sammi and then back to Blake and shook my head. "Stop being a dick. We get it, you think you're awesome, but really you're just lucky. And luck always runs out."

The guys who were standing by and witnessed the whole thing winced at my words and then laughed when Sammi tried to defend Blake. For the last month I had avoided him, and in the span of a few hours I had not only faced him, but stood up to him. I knew he was embarrassed, but that was no longer my problem. If he wanted to be a jerk to me, that was one thing, but Meg was the kindest and most gracious person I knew—there was no way I would let him disrespect her.

"What did I miss?" Colin asked as he walked in, an angry Blake pushing past him.

"Not much," I said. "Where's Chris?"

"Right here," Chris said as he walked in and gave me a hug. He pointed over his shoulder where Blake and Sammie had passed him. "What crawled up Blake's ass?"

"What didn't?" Deacon, one of the other football players, asked with a laugh.

I looked around, waiting for someone to let us in on the secret. It was pretty obvious something—more than me telling him off—was bothering Blake.

Marcus raised a brow at Deacon before looking at me and shook his head. "You didn't hear?"

"Clearly," I mused.

"The other day in the locker room, Blake told Coach that he would've gotten a full ride if the rest of the team would've played better."

"He didn't," I gasped. "You're joking."

"Heard it myself," Marcus said. "I was this close to punching him."

"You and everyone else in the room," Deacon said. "I don't think he realized we were right outside Coach's office when he said it. He walked out like nothing happened."

"That's awful, guys. I'm so sorry."

"Not like you said it," Marcus said with a shrug. "Guess you learn exactly who people are when you're not around."

Blake and Sammie were huddled together in the living room talking to a couple of people when he looked my way. His shoulders stooped, and all I could do was shrug. The guy I knew before was fun and energetic, always the center of attention. But that Blake was gone, and clearly replaced with the worst version of himself.

I turned back to see Meg and Knox walking back into the kitchen area. She was smiling so wide as she talked to Knox, who looked equally happy. When I caught her eye, she said something to him and hurried over to me excitedly.

"Well that only took you four years," I teased.

Meg slapped my shoulder playfully and linked her arm with mine as she dragged me toward the back yard. Once we were a safe distance away, she let out a quiet squeal as she tried to contain herself.

"He asked me out."

"Really? That's great!"

"I know. I'm so excited. I played it cool...at least I think I did. But whatever, he asked me out."

"Good for you," I said, squeezing her hand.

"But that's not why I dragged you over here."

"No? Then why?"

Meg looked out the window where some of our classmates had gathered outside. I was waiting to see what else she said, but instead she waved me to look out the window. There were easily fifty people outside, but she was pointing to the one who was sitting near the pool with a few of his friends.

"Milo's here," she said quietly. "You should go talk to him."

CHAPTER 3

MILO

Holland Monroe had been in at least one of my classes every year since we were freshmen. She always wore her brown curly hair in a ponytail, like it was her trademark. The few times she wore it down, she looked self-conscious for some reason, but I could never seem to not look at her. And she'd never looked more confident and beautiful as she did when we ran into each other at graduation.

I had tried to get up the nerve to talk to her more times than I would care to admit. Each time ended with me staring at her and making some face that seemingly made her laugh. And though it was never my intention, I liked her laugh. It seemed that I could talk to just about anyone—except Holland.

I had heard conversations she had with people, and one of the things I noticed was how nice she was to everyone. If you asked our classmates about her, most of them would have something kind to say about her. Even despite my awkwardness when it came to formulating a sentence around her, she would still smile and try to talk to me. That was usually interrupted by the teacher who was lecturing, but it never went unnoticed by me. Besides, it seemed that I always came off sounding like a jerk anyway.

But the day came that I finally got up the nerve to talk to her in the hallway, with the pretense of getting together to study. Senior year came—yes, senior year—and I had it all planned out. We had AP psych together, and Mr. Johnson liked to assign group projects. All I had to do was talk to her to see if she wanted to partner up with me. And then I saw her with Blake Cohen, the varsity quarterback. They were standing near the lockers, talking, and as I got closer I realized they were holding hands. He bent down and kissed her before shoving off the lockers and walked her to her class.

For a moment I thought she had seen me, but if she did, it didn't matter. The next five months were spent with people talking about Holland and Blake and how cute they were together. But Blake had always been a conceited ass, and I figured that meant Holland may have joined the ranks of asses too.

"What are you looking at?" Ethan, my best friend, asked.

I had not realized I was staring until he called me out, and then I wondered if anyone else noticed. It wasn't hard to notice Holland when we walked into any gathering. At least not for me.

"Nothing," I muttered. "I thought I saw Wes."

"He texted a bit ago. He's not coming," Ethan said. "How long do you want to stick around?"

Ethan, Daryl, Hunter, and I had decided we would make a brief stop by Knox's party before going over to Daryl's girlfriend's house. The only reason I agreed to go to Knox's was on the off chance I would get to see Holland one last time. I had no idea what her plans were for the summer or college in the fall, though I had heard she was accepted to Westview University.

Of course, when she spoke to me after the graduation ceremony, I had managed to be struck mute. Again. And when she spoke, questioning why I disliked her, I wanted to kick my own ass. It always took me a bit of time to warm up to people. My personality was not incredibly engaging, and my sense of humor—not for everyone. So it was understandable that she found it hard to see me beyond that facade.

"I'm in no rush," I said, to answer his question. "Y'all tell me when you're ready."

"Thanks for being the DD tonight," Hunter said as he raised his beer.

"No problem," I laughed.

I was not much for drinking. When I was younger, Dad would have the occasional beer, but after Mom died, they were few and far between. Anytime the guys wanted to go out, I would usually offer to drive, and they were more than willing to accept.

"Hey Holland," Daryl called out when he noticed her walking out of the back door.

She spotted him and smiled as she waved. A gust of wind blew her curly hair in every direction, but she didn't seem to care. I wanted to smack Daryl for calling her over, but I was enjoying the view. Besides, no one was aware of the feelings I had had for Holland for nearly four years.

"Hey, Daryl," she said as she walked over and hugged him. She hugged my other two friends and then looked at me, nodding her greeting. "Hey, Milo."

"Hi, Holland."

She smiled and then gave her attention to Hunter when he asked about her day. I found myself fully engaged, listening to everything she said, down to the part about being the designated driver for Meg.

"No kidding," Hunter laughed. "Milo is our DD."

"Really?" she asked.

"Someone has to babysit these idiots," I deadpanned.

The guys laughed, but she looked stunned or put off by what I had said. I wanted to tell her that I was joking—hell, I thought it was obvious by the fact that the guys were laughing.

"I'm gonna grab another one," Hunter said. "Daryl? Ethan?"

"I'll come with," Ethan said, and Daryl agreed.

The three walked off in search of more beer, leaving me alone with Holland. We stood in painfully awkward silence for what felt like hours. I guess she felt the same, because she looked around and waved at a few people she knew. I was willing myself to say something to get her stay and talk to me, but my mouth refused to cooperate.

"Well, I guess I better get back to Meg. Good seeing you again," she said with a disappointed smile.

"You too," I managed to say, but it was too late. She was already gone.

"I don't hate you. You look beautiful," I mumbled under my breath.

"Who are you talking to?" Ethan asked.

"I wasn't talking."

"Where'd Holland go?" he asked.

"Back inside."

"Did you talk to her?"

I shook my head and he rolled his eyes.

"Man. You're joking right? I know you have a thing for her..."

I shook my head and opened my mouth to object but he silenced me with a glare.

"That's why I walked away, to give you some time alone. And you didn't talk to her?"

"She had to go find Meg."

"Is this how your life is gonna be? Just letting everything pass you by and never taking chances?"

"I take plenty of chances," I reminded him. "I applied to five colleges all over the country."

"And yet you're staying in Pine Bridge. Why?"

Getting into the details of why I was staying in my hometown was not on my agenda. I had other things going on, and there was no way I would justify my decisions to him or anyone else. Ethan was my closest friend, but that did not mean I told him everything. I was deliberate in every choice I made, and that had worked for me so far.

"That's what I thought," he said before taking a swig of beer. "Just so you know, girls like her don't stay single for long."

"What am I supposed to do with that?" I scoffed.

"That's up to you. So what's it gonna be?"

Holland walked back into Knox's house, ending my opportunity to talk to her. Ethan was about to say something when Melanie, a friend of mine, joined us.

"Hey, Mel," I said, giving her a hug when she was closer. "How's it going?"

"Not bad. What about you?"

"Same."

"He lies," Ethan scoffed.

"What's going on?" she asked.

"Nothing," I warned through gritted teeth, but Ethan ignored me and turned his attention back to Mel.

"Let me ask you something," he said.

"Shoot."

"Say you like someone. What would you do about it?"

She crossed her arms over her chest and looked between the two of us questioningly. I shrugged my shoulders and Mel smiled.

"I'd talk to him. See if maybe there was any clue that he felt the same way…probably drop a few hints here and there."

"So, you're telling me you wouldn't avoid the guy? Ignore him?"

"Not if I actually wanted a chance with him," she laughed.

Ethan hit my chest and pointed at Mel. "See? That right there."

"Okay, I answered your question. Does someone want to explain?" she asked.

"It's Milo. He doesn't know how to talk to girls."

"He talks to me," she answered.

"Let me rephrase that: he can't talk to girls he likes."

"Well gee, thanks, Ethan," she mumbled.

"That's not what I mean," he protested.

Mel ignored him and turned her attention to me. "So who's the girl?"

"No one."

"Holland," Ethan answered for me.

"Holland? Really? She's great! Why don't you talk to her?"

"I talk to her," I defended.

"Yeah, he talks to her. About projects and crap like that. I gave him the perfect opportunity to have alone time not even ten minutes ago, and he screwed that up."

Mel's shoulders sagged and she looked at me with complete disappointment. "What did you do?"

"Nothing."

"He's not lying," Ethan laughed.

"All right Ethan. Go way," she said, waving him off. "I need to talk to Milo."

Ethan grinned and walked off, leaving me alone with Mel. When he was a good distance away, she turned her attention to me and I knew that she was about to lecture me.

"Holland is one of the nicest people."

"I know."

"Okay, so then you know that she can and will talk to anyone."

"Yeah, well, I can't talk to her. Believe me, I've tried. But when I have the chance, it's like something just happens. My mind goes blank and words don't come out. I try to come up with something to say, some way to get her to talk to me, but I fail every time."

"You're trying too hard. Just let it happen naturally."

"You don't think I've tried? There's just something about her that intimidates the hell out of me. And that was my chance to talk to her."

"She and I talk. Want me to put in a good word for you? Bring her out here to talk to you?"

"No," I objected too forcefully.

"If you change your mind, let me know."

"Thanks, Mel."

We stood quiet and looked over the crowd that had gathered at Knox's house. Mel was always up for anything. There weren't many people who were as easygoing as her, which was one of the reasons my friends were always trying to date her. But she never gave any of them the time of day.

"Can I ask you something?" Her voice sounded nervous, something I was not used to hearing from her. I turned to face her and she wore a shy smile.

"Do you think it would be a mistake if I went out with Hunter?"

"You like Hunter?"

I turned my head toward the keg, where he was talking to Ethan and a few others, before looking at her again. Mel pursed her lips together and nodded.

"I thought you rejected him already."

"I did. But he sure is persistent."

I laughed loud and wrapped an arm around her, hugging her. "He wore you down?"

"What can I say? He stepped up. Made sure that I knew he was interested." She looked up at me and winked.

"Are you trying to tell me something?"

Instead of answering my question, she stood on her toes and kissed my cheek before walking over to Hunter. He saw her approaching and smiled when she reached for his hand. I envied both of them; they knew what they wanted and went for it.

CHAPTER 4

HOLLAND

I woke up in the morning berating myself for staying out so late. When we got to Meg's house, her parents were already in bed, but I knew they were waiting up for us. By the time we got in bed, it was three in the morning and I had to work later in the day.

Meg was still sleeping when I got up, so I grabbed my stuff and went home in hopes of grabbing a few blissful hours of sleep before my shift. But when I got home, my parents were working around the house and pleaded with me to help. Before I knew it, I only had thirty minutes to shower and dress so I could make it to work on time.

I needed caffeine and about four more hours of sleep, but I did my best to look up for the work. When I walked into Pine Bridge Country Club, I was greeted by an older woman with blond hair, her outfit pristine, not a wrinkle to be found. As soon as I saw her, I knew she had to be Ms. Hendricks, the club manager. I straightened my back and did my best to exude confidence and professionalism.

"You must be Holland," Ms. Hendricks said as she breezed

past me.

"Yes ma'am," I answered, following after her.

"We have a busy day today, so there's no time to train you. I need you on the floor. If you have any questions, you can talk to Daphne."

She pushed open the kitchen door and I had to grab it before it swung backward and hit me. There were people rushing about in the large kitchen, and as we walked through them, she pointed to a woman with short black hair.

"That's Daphne."

I attempted a wave, but Daphne was busy making notes on a piece of paper. She lifted her eyes only momentarily and went back to her work. I began to regret my choice of working at the country club, but dutifully followed along anyway. I had never been a quitter—at least not on my first day.

When we reached Ms. Hendricks' office, she grabbed a pressed white button-down shirt emblazoned with the Pine Bridge logo. I held it up and smiled.

When I was a kid, my parents took us to eat at the restaurant for their fifteenth wedding anniversary. Everyone looked so polished, and the dining area was fancier than anything else I had seen. And it was my turn to work in the place I always regarded as *the* best.

"Well?"

"I'm sorry?" I looked up, seeing my new boss staring at me.

Ms. Hendricks rolled her eyes. "Go get changed."

"Yes."

I hurried to the small restroom down the hall and quickly changed into the shirt, tucking it in neatly. She had told me to wear black slacks when we had talked before, so I was prepared for that. But I was not ready to wait tables at the nicest restaurant in Pine Bridge. At least not without some training.

I walked back into her office and she looked up from her desk, eyeing me from top to bottom. I knew she was checking out my appearance, and I felt vulnerable under her scrutiny. She nodded once and pointed to the chair across from where she sat.

"This is your card. Swipe when you come in, when you take your breaks, and when you leave. Now, for some ground rules—no visible tattoos may show, no piercings, no crazy hair colors. Do you understand?"

"Yes ma'am."

"I realize that things come up, so if you can give me a heads-up if you are unable to work before I do the schedule, that would be helpful. *If* you are scheduled and you cannot make it, it is your responsibly to find a replacement for that shift. Do you understand?"

"Yes."

"You may find that you are working the patio grill bistro outside by the pool—on those days, you are to wear khaki shorts and a short-sleeved shirt that I will give you before you leave tonight. When you are wearing the club logo, you are to conduct yourself in a professional manner at all times because you are representing the club."

She sat back in her chair and looked at me over her glasses. She had said so much so fast and I was still taking it in, though none of it was rocket science. Ms. Hendricks ran a tight ship and I wanted to impress her.

"Do you have any questions?"

"Just a couple," I said, and she nodded for me to continue. "When will the chef provide details about the specials? And is it okay to carry a cheat sheet for that?"

"Specials are only offered in the evenings, and Chef will let you know an hour before we open for dinner. I'd prefer you memorize the specials, but I'll let it slide for the first few shifts. Talk to Daphne—she has some tips to help with that."

"Okay." I stood up, ready to go back to the kitchen, when she started to speak again.

"When you are not working, you are allowed to use the

facilities at a discounted rate. However, the pool is available free of charge."

It was on the tip of my tongue to tell her the pool was the only thing I was interested in, but I thought better of it and nodded my understanding.

"Thank you, Ms. Hendricks."

"Don't thank me, Holland—impress me."

She looked down at the paperwork in front of her, dismissing me from her presence. I took a deep breath and walked back toward the kitchen, making sure that my shirt was properly tucked along the way. There were still several people moving about, and I walked toward Daphne, who was talking to one of the cooks.

"You're the new girl," she said, reaching out her hand. "I'm Daphne. Assistant manager."

"Holland. Nice to meet you."

She smiled and handed me a slip of paper. "You missed the specials, so here they are. Memorize them."

As I read the list, my stomach began to growl, reminding me that I had forgotten to grab a snack before I left home. Daphne, if she heard it, ignored the sound and continued talking.

"Let me show you around the kitchen and introduce you to some of the people here."

We walked to a heavyset man with graying hair who was busy stirring something in a pot. He was clean-shaven and had a few wrinkles on his face that made him look older than my dad.

"This is Carlo, but Hendricks calls him Chef."

"I don't like being called Chef," he said, lifting his eyes to see me.

"Nice to meet you." I smiled. "Holland."

"That is our sous-chef Jaysen," Daphne said, pointing to another man, who was younger than Carlo. Jaysen had a chiseled jawline, dark skin, and was thin and muscular. I could tell by the two waitresses talking to him that he was a hot commodity.

Daphne leaned toward me and muttered, "He's beautiful."

All I could do was nod in agreement.

"We have a pastry chef and a grill chef, but there're busy right now. You'll meet them later. And then we have a kitchen assistant somewhere. Has anyone seen…"

"Holland?" I heard a voice say nearby. It was familiar, but I was not able to place it until I turned and saw him in his white coat.

"Milo?"

His arms were full of kitchen items that he was close to dropping. He turned away from me and walked to where Carlo stood and set them down.

"Oh good. You two know each other," Daphne said before walking to a small machine mounted to the wall. "And over here is where you'll check in."

She had already walked away, and I started to follow her when I looked back at Milo, who was busy with other tasks. I shook my head and walked to Daphne so I could check in for my first shift.

"I'm sure Hendricks told you that we're busy tonight, so we're gonna have to drop you in the deep end. You okay with that?"

I huffed a sarcastic laugh. "Okay? Not sure. But I've waited tables before, so I'm sure it'll be fine."

Daphne patted my shoulder once. "There ya go."

We walked back to the main kitchen area and she cleared her throat. "All right everyone, gather 'round."

The cooks continued working while the waitstaff stopped to listen to Daphne. She spoke quickly, giving directions about who had which sections, reminding them of the specials, and something about an employee night out.

"Oh, before I forget, this is the new girl—Holland. If you could all introduce yourselves when you have a moment, that would be great."

I noticed that Milo looked up briefly from his work and looked in my direction, but went right back to his task. I returned my attention to Daphne, who was speaking to me again.

"If you have any questions, any problems, just ask someone here. Guys, if you see she needs help, step up. Okay? All right, let's get out there and make sure everything is ready before the first guests come in."

Everyone walked off, a few of them introducing themselves as they passed me.

"I'm Brandon," a blond-haired, tan-skinned, muscularly built guy said as he stood in front of me. His smile revealed dimpled cheeks that fit the guy-next-door image.

He was handsome, but something about the way he approached me reminded me a little too much of Blake. It was almost an instant dislike, but I knew that was neither rational nor fair. I needed to remember that not everyone would disappoint me like Blake had.

"Holland," I said with a smile, taking his offered hand and shaking it. "Nice to meet you."

"Why don't I show you your section and help you get ready for tonight?"

"Sounds good," I said, following him through the kitchen doors.

The restaurant tables were set with white tablecloths and a single candle lit in the middle. The place settings were already laid out, but missing the utensils.

"Here," Brandon said. He picked up a tub full of silverware and I followed him. "We need to set these out. Every night, it's someone else's turn. So tonight's our night."

"*Our* turn?"

"Well, we have...*teams*—and you're on mine."

34

I glanced around at the others who were setting up, and it seemed like most were working alone. It was on the tip of my tongue to ask, but instead I began to take the napkin-wrapped bundles of silverware and place them on the tables while he explained the sections. I appreciated his time and attention, because without it I would have been more lost than I was at the moment.

When we were done, Brandon stood next to me with his arms crossed. He inched slightly closer, nudged my arm, and smiled. I shifted my weight to gain a bit of breathing room as he told me more about the dinner rush and some tips for working with some of the regulars. I appreciated the information, but the one thing I didn't like was how he kept brushing up against me, or touching my arm for random reasons.

"I'm sure I'll be fine," I said. "Thanks for the help."

Brandon looked down at me and grinned as he leaned in again. I don't care how attractive someone is, personal space is personal space—and Brandon was breaching mine. I stepped forward to gain some space and cleared my throat.

"So is there anything else I need to do?"

He shook his head and shrugged. "Nah. We just wait. And remember, Carlo might snap at you, but he means well, so don't take it personal."

"I don't mind," I said.

Snappish words and cold shoulders didn't hurt me. I'd been on the receiving end of both for as long as I could remember, and most recently from Milo—who apparently would be my co-worker.

***

An hour into the dinner rush, I was lost, flustered, and barely making it. But barely making it wasn't the same as completely failing.

Daphne and Brandon both stepped up and helped by bringing trays of food out to my tables and refilling glasses of water while they were attending to their own tables. I knew there were things I needed to work on, but for the most part it seemed that everything went smoothly. By the end of my shift, I was so tired that my eyes were beginning to burn.

I took off my apron and wrapped my tablet inside before shoving it into the small cubby I was assigned. I went to see Hendricks to get my other shirt before leaving for the night, and as I walked to the exit, I heard Milo call out to me.

"You didn't clock out," he said.

My feet were killing me, I was certain I smelled like a ten-year-old boy who didn't know how to use deodorant, and I was more tired than I had been in years. So when Milo spoke up, I was grateful for the help.

"Thanks," I said before making my way to swipe my card.

I noticed a stack of dishes on the counter, so I picked them up and placed them in the sink. I knew that Milo was standing nearby, working on whatever it was that Carlo needed him to do, but I didn't move right away. A part of me hoped that Milo would actually speak to me. His quiet infuriated me, but not as much as it insulted me. For some reason, I wanted him—I needed him—to like me. And it was clear that everything about me was a disappointment to Milo.

"How was your first day?" he asked, still unwilling or unable to look at me.

"Exhausting."

"It gets better. Just make sure to do everything Hendricks and Daphne told you and you'll be fine."

"Are you actually speaking me?" I asked teasingly. "Is Milo Davis being nice?"

He stopped what he was doing and turned to face me, his brows pinched together in question.

"Am I not nice?" he asked.

I shrugged. "Not to me, you're not."

He turned around to fully face me and leaned against the counter with his arms crossed over his chest. I could tell that my words struck him in a way I did not expect. In fact, I was surprised—because surely someone had called him out before.

"How am I mean?"

"I didn't say you're *mean*. But you're definitely not approachable."

One side of his mouth quirked up in a tight smile, and as much as I wanted to look away, I couldn't. Seeing him looking slightly embarrassed, like he had never heard anything like that before, was charming.

"*I'm* not approachable? Pot—kettle."

"Are you implying that I'm not?" I asked. The shift in the conversation, the fact that we were having an actual conversation, had me stumped.

"I don't know about you, but I think we had a great conversation last night," he said in monotone.

A burst of laughter escaped my mouth and he looked offended. I felt bad because he had stunned me with his bluntness, but I was not laughing at *him*.

"Forget it," he said as he started to turn back around, but I reached out for his arm to stop him. He resumed his position, still apprehensive about talking to me, based on his closed-off body language.

"I'm not laughing at you—per se. I'm laughing at what you said."

"Because that's so much better?"

"No, it's just that, I thought the same thing. I don't think we've ever really talked. You rarely talked to me in class, and if you saw me, it's like you'd rather look anywhere else, and forget about the group projects—good grief, I mean, if looks could kill."

"What are you talking about?"

"Jeez, Milo! Even at graduation, when I ran into you, you looked at me like I was a leper."

"First of all, I don't talk if I don't have anything to say."

"And second?" I asked, crossing my arms over my chest, mimicking his stance.

"It takes two to have a conversation, and you never seemed interested."

We both stood in silence, allowing the words we had spoken to reach the intended target. Honestly, I had never considered that the reason he didn't talk to me was because I didn't initiate a conversation. But then again, he never seemed to care enough to try either.

"You're an intimidating person," I finally said.

"How so?"

"I never said anything to you because you seemed like you hate the world. Every part of you is closed off."

"Maybe it's just you."

Ouch!

"Well, I could say the same thing."

"It's me?"

"Your friends didn't have a problem talking to me…They never have. I walked over there to talk to you. Hell, I hoped that maybe you would say something, attempt a conversation, make small talk. I mean, would it kill you to be nice to me? I've racked my brain trying to figure out what it is about me that you hate so much."

Milo's mouth slowly turned up, a smile playing on his lips. He was actually looking at me, for maybe the first time, like I wasn't a pariah.

"What are you smiling about? Was something I said funny?"

"No," he answered.

"Then why are you smiling?"

"What you just said."

"That it's you?"

"No. The other thing."

"Can you be more specific?"

"You wanted to talk to me."

"Well, yeah. We had classes together...worked together."

"That's not what you said."

I thought back on my defensive rant, wondering what I had said, and then it hit me. My cheeks began to grow warm, and I knew it probably showed in the form of redness. Milo still wore his smile, like he was in on a secret.

"Why are you smiling like that?" I asked.

"Because you wanted to talk to me."

I walked myself into that one, but instead of giving him what he was looking for, I turned around to walk off. "I liked it better when you were quiet," I lied.

"It was just you," he called out as I continued walking away.

I didn't bother to answer him, because anything I said could be flipped around and I'd be left looking like an even bigger idiot.

I went into the small closet that doubled as a storage area for employee items and grabbed my purse before clocking out for the day. I had only been working for one day, but it felt like months. It was fast paced, and there was not much time to twiddle your thumbs because there was always something to do. Daphne told me it would only get worse as the summer went on, which didn't make me feel any better.

CHAPTER 5

HOLLAND

By the time I worked my second shift, things felt a little more natural to me. There was still a lot to learn and figure out, but mostly I liked the work. The timing was not the best, mainly because Meg would be leaving in just a few days and not only had I not spent any time with her, I was not ready to let her go.

When my phone buzzed in my hand, I knew who it was before I even looked at the screen.

Meg: Are you coming?
Me: I just got off work. I'll be there.

I dreaded going to her house because it meant I would be saying goodbye. She was flying out at the end of the weekend and this would be her final farewell. The bad thing was I would have to say goodbye with fifty other people, so I knew my time with her would not be what either of us wanted.

Once my phone was tucked away, I walked through the kitchen, keeping my eyes from wandering to where I knew Milo would be standing. We had not talked since my first night at work, but there had been more eye contact and random smiles that I was not used to receiving from him.

Luckily, I saw Daphne talking to one of the other waiters and I turned to say my goodbyes as I walked outside into the warm summer evening. It was already dark out, and the uniform I wore for work felt like it was sticking to my skin under the heat of the night.

"See ya," Milo said, startling me.

"Crap! You scared the shit out of me!" I yelled as I turned and spotted him near a car under a parking lot light.

"You should always be aware of your surroundings," he reprimanded.

"Jeez, you sound like my mom," I laughed, but he didn't seem entertained by my comment. "Goodnight, Milo."

I walked to my car, discreetly making sure I was aware of what was going on so that he didn't know I took his words to heart. When I unlocked the door, I tossed my purse inside and looked up to see him still watching me, so I waved.

"It was you," he said, loud enough for me to hear him.

I was about to get into my car when he said those words and I stopped moving.

"That I didn't talk to. It was just you."

I slammed my door shut and walked toward him, fury pushing each of my steps. I was about twenty feet away from him, close enough to see his expression, far enough that he could not touch me. Not that I was afraid of Milo—I was far too annoyed to be afraid.

"What did I ever do to you to make you hate me?" I asked. My voice sounded pained to my own ears and I knew why. I wanted people to like me, and I hated to know that they didn't.

"I don't hate you."

"But you just said—"

"I said that I didn't talk to you. You just assumed the worst."

He took a tentative step toward me and I remained fixed in

41

place. Curiosity would not let me walk away, though that was exactly what I wanted to do. He stood across from me, the annoyance and disgust erased from his face. Milo shoved his hands into his pockets and when he looked up at me, he looked— uncertain.

"I didn't know how to talk to you," he finally said.

"You don't seem to have a problem now," I snapped. "In fact, I sort of wish you'd go back to ignoring me."

"If that's what you want…"

"No, Milo, that's not what I want. I want to understand."

"You're not really that naïve, are you?"

"Forget it," I said, turning around to walk back to my car.

"I never talked to you because I didn't know how to," he said, but I kept walking. "Because I liked you."

That was the thing he said that got me to stop moving. In fact, I was pretty sure that I heard him wrong, so I slowly turned around to give him my attention. I didn't know what to say.

"I didn't know how to talk to you without sounding like a moron, so I just…*didn't*…talk. You really didn't know?"

"You said it yourself: you didn't talk to me. So your silence spoke volumes for you."

"I'm sorry," he said. "I'm just not much of a talker anyway, and then it's you…"

"Me?"

"I wasn't trying to be a jerk the other night. I just didn't know what to say to you."

"I didn't know what to say to you either. Every time I've tried to talk to you, it's like talking to a brick wall. No matter how hard I try or how nice I am to you, you just ignore me."

"That was never my intention," he said apologetically. "I really just didn't know what to say."

We stood in silence, each really hearing the other. His confession began to ring in my ears, and I was thankful for the darkness so he would not see my flushed cheeks.

"Did you mean what you said?"

"Which part?"

"That you liked me?"

He shifted his stance before facing me again. "Yeah. I did...I do."

"Really?"

"Really."

Milo was completely opposite of Blake, or anyone else I had dated. He was not the center of attention, and he was not cocky. He was shy and unassuming, and for so long I had wanted to get him to open up and let me be his friend. I never expected him to open up so much that he would reveal that he had feelings for me.

"If you aren't busy, do you want to go get something to eat? Maybe we could actually talk or something?"

"Are you asking me out on a date?" I asked.

He looked away for a moment, and when his gaze connected with mine, his smile grew. "Yeah. I guess I am."

I felt nervous and excited at the same time, and then complete disappointment.

"I can't. Not tonight," I said.

"No. It's fine. Short notice and all. Hell, you might be dating someone anyway."

"I'm not," I said a little more eagerly than I realized.

"Maybe another time," he said, taking a few steps backward. "Have a good night, Holland."

As he turned around, I slowly did the same, but then my feet stopped moving.

"Do you want to come with me?" I asked hopefully. "To Meg's?"

"Meg's?"

"It's her going-away party. She's having some people over."

"That's probably not a good idea."

"Why?"

"I don't want to intrude."

"You said yourself I was the only person you didn't talk to…unless you liked everyone."

"No," he laughed softly.

"Then prove it," I said. "Come with me."

"Can I change my clothes?" he asked. "I'd rather not smell like the kitchen."

"Yeah. I need to do the same."

"So I'll pick you up in an hour?" he asked.

I swallowed hard and pursed my lips together, trying to keep my elated smile from showing. I had had a crush on Milo for some time, but I had never allowed myself to admit it to anyone. Not even Meg.

"Okay," I agreed as I walked to my car.

"Hey, Holland?"

I stopped and looked at him, realizing he was closer than I thought. He stayed a safe distance away, but had his phone in his hand, stretched out to me. I looked at the device and then at him.

"I need your number so I can text you to get your address."

"Oh, yeah," I laughed, taking it from his hand. I put my number into his phone and gave it back to him. He stepped away and smiled as he waited for me to get into my car.

When I drove away, I looked in my rearview mirror and saw him pump his fist into the air and I started laughing, feeling my cheeks burn from the enormous smile on my face.

***

"You're finally here," Meg shouted when she opened the door. Her excitement soon morphed into shock when she saw Milo standing next to me. "Hey, Milo. Glad you could make it."

My eyes widened, as if to tell her to shut up, and she stepped aside, her smile fully in place.

"We are talking later," she muttered when she hugged me.

I knew we would talk, even if she wouldn't have said so; I needed the conversation.

Milo had arrived at my house early enough to walk to the door and meet my parents—something Blake never did.

When I had finished changing, I was walking toward the living room and I found Milo talking with Ben and my dad about baseball. Ben played in college and followed the sport closely, so for him to have someone to talk to about it was a big deal.

I listened in from hallway and found it amusing how easily he fell into conversation with my family. Yet with me, he was so quiet.

When I finally walked into the room, there was a flutter in my chest at seeing him sitting so comfortably near my dad. Milo stood up and those flutters traveled to my stomach. He was wearing a white T-shirt with a plaid shirt over it, the sleeves rolled up, and a pair of dark jeans. Milo Davis was standing in my living room, looking at me the way I had always wanted someone to look at me.

And thirty minutes later, we were at Meg's house—together.

"Can I get you anything to drink?" Meg asked Milo.

"Nah. I'm good. Thanks."

"Okay. Well, Holland knows where everything is, so if you need anything, she's your girl."

Realizing the innuendo in her words, Meg pursed her lips together and stifled a smile. If she had been standing next to me, I would have elbowed her in the stomach or something equally painful. But no, she was standing a safe distance away.

"C'mon, we're all outside."

Milo waited for me to follow Meg and then fell into step with me.

"Hey Holland. Hey Milo," Knox said.

I looked at him and then at Meg, who was trying to bite back a smile. She had neglected to tell me that Knox would be at her house. And from the way they were standing so close, it looked like there might have been something going on between them.

"Hey," I said, giving him a hug. "How's it going?"

"Not bad. Sucks that Meg is leaving in a couple of days, though."

"Yeah. No kidding. Overachiever," I teased. "She just had to show all of us up, didn't she?"

Meg looked at Milo and pulled him into the conversation. "So what are you two doing together?"

"Wow, blunt," I scoffed.

Milo smiled and shrugged his shoulders. "I asked her out."

She laughed and high-fived him. "Nice."

"About time," Knox deadpanned, and I looked at him in shock. He smirked and cocked his head to the side. "Really, Holland? You didn't know?"

"Yeah, this is the face of someone in the know," I said, pointing to myself.

"Aw, she's cute when she's clueless," Meg teased.

"Shut up," I said, rolling my eyes. "You're one to talk."

Meg's eyes grew wide, and with a tight shake of the head that only I noticed, I dropped the subject. I guess she had not yet admitted to Knox that she had had a thing for him for the last four years.

"Why don't we get something to drink?" I asked, taking ahold of Milo's arm.

He gave me a questioning look and then simply nodded his head. "Yeah, I'm thirsty."

As we walked away, Milo leaned in to ask a question at the same time I turned toward him to explain what was going on. I was caught off guard by the closeness, and realized I was no longer moving. Neither of us were moving. In the last five hours, we had spoken more than we had in all the years we had known each other. And in the last five seconds, my heart had started beating so fast I could feel my pulse ticking in my neck.

By the way his eyes dilated when he looked at me, I could tell he felt the something too. I cleared my throat and took a deep breath as I tried to gain my composure. But there was no quieting the voice inside my head that was beginning to scream for Milo.

"Sorry," I muttered.

"It's fine…I was just…" He pointed toward the house.

"Food?"

"Yeah. I could eat."

We walked toward the house and I explained the situation with Meg and Knox and the reason for her silencing me. He laughed, but commented that they looked like they were enjoying each other's company.

"I'm glad you asked me to come," he said when we walked inside the Clarkes' home.

"Me, too."

Milo and I spent most of the evening walking around and talking to friends and classmates that Meg had invited to her party. I found myself quietly watching him when we were not together, and it was then that I noticed how talkative he was with everyone.

Everyone but me.

"So who's the guy?" Meg's mom asked when she walked over to me.

"Milo Davis."

"And is Milo Davis a boyfriend? I noticed that you two walked in together."

I smiled and shook my head. "No, Mrs. Clarke…he's not a boyfriend. Just a classmate."

"Classmate, huh?" she teased. "If you say so."

CHAPTER 6

MILO

We were the last ones to leave Meg's party, and I could see that it was weighing heavy on Holland's shoulders. The two of them had always been inseparable. If you wanted to find Holland, all you had to do was look for Meg and there she would be, no more than five feet away. That was my go-to, anyway.

Meg was nice to everyone but incredibly shy. But that was something that she seemed to be working on, because not only did she corner me and ask about Holland, she had also gotten up the nerve to ask Knox out on a date.

"So you finally talked to her?" Meg asked when she found me in the kitchen grabbing a drink.

I wanted to play it cool, pretend I didn't know what she was talking about, but she just smiled and waited for my answer.

"Yeah."

"And?"

"Well, we argued at first."

"Argued?"

"It was more like being defensive, I guess."

"But you're here, with her, so that must mean something."

I didn't need to respond because that part was obvious. For most of the night, I had watched her with Meg's family and envied how easily everyone else related to her. Holland was someone I always wanted to get to know, but I had never been able to just put myself out there. When she had invited me to go to Meg's party, as much as I wanted to stick with my original answer, I reconsidered because I would get to step some one-on-one time with her. I needed to know if I had built up the idea of Holland in my head, or if maybe she was really as awesome as I thought.

"So what happens now?" Meg asked.

"What do you mean?"

"Well, she leaves for Westview in August. Is this going to be a summer fling thing? Are you going to try a long-distance relationship?"

"Meg?" I asked, stopping her before her list of questions continued to grow.

"Yeah?"

"We haven't even gone out on a date," I said with a chuckle.

She bit her lip to keep from smiling at what she had just thrown at me, but it did little to help.

"Okay, fair enough, but that's something you need to think about. I don't want to see either of you hurt."

"We might go out and find out we're just good friends."

"Is that what you're hoping for?"

Hope?

I didn't know how to answer that, for a variety of reasons. Hope implied faith, or belief, and I wasn't sure I was capable of either of those anymore.

"I just want to get to know her. How's that?"

"It's a good start." She grinned before looking outside. "I'm going to get her to stay here tonight. You can take her home or whatever, but she and I need to have a talk…about you."

"Why does that make me nervous?"

"It shouldn't, because I'm on your side here. I think you two would be really good together. So I'm going to give her a little push."

"Meg, I appreciate it, I do. But if she decides to go out with me, or even possibly date me, I want it to be because she's interested, not because someone pushed her into it."

She nodded and started to walk out of the kitchen, but paused and looked back at me. "She'd kill me if she knew I said anything, but I'm pretty sure she's interested."

Meg walked back outside and I was once again alone in the kitchen. I looked through the window and saw Holland talking to some people. She threw her head back in laughter and I felt my own smile grow. I don't know how our argument earlier at work had ended with me being at a party with her, but I was thanking whatever forces had made that happen.

***

When I got home after dropping her off, I stayed in my car in the driveway and thought about Holland. I had built her up so much in my mind that I had been too nervous to talk to her. Now that we had spent some time together, I really wanted to get to know her better. I pulled out my phone and texted her.

Me: Busy?

Holland: Just watching Pretty in Pink

Me: OK. Well, just wanted to say thanks for letting me tag along tonight.

Holland: I had fun

Me: Me too. We should do it again

Holland: Go to a party?

I laughed to myself as I tried to think of something witty to say, but I fell short. I wanted to make *her* laugh—she had a great laugh. I wanted to make enough of an impression that when she saw me, she could not help but smile.

Me: No. Hang out.

As I waited for a response, hoping that she would want to see me again outside of work, I wondered where I could take her that would impress her. Holland had dated a number of guys in school, and all of them were completely opposite of me. She had dated the jock, and the cut-up, the slacker, and the all-American guy next door. Not to discount my strong points, because I knew what those were. I needed to stand out. Finally, after waiting for a response, three little dots appeared on the screen and then I read her text to me.

Holland: Can't wait. Let me know when and I'll be there.

I knew she was probably already back at Meg's, so I typed out one last text before I got out of my car. I was in a much better place than when I had left to pick her up. I had been so worried I would make an ass of myself, but her dad and brother had made me feel welcome while I waited for her and taken the pressure off.

I walked inside the house and closed the door quietly behind me so I would not wake Dad. He was would be getting up soon for work since he was on nights, and he needed the rest.

"You're late," Dad snapped when I walked through the kitchen.

The good mood I was in after my night with Holland started to sour at the sound of his tone. He never made a big deal about curfew, but then again, it was not often that I went out. Dad was sitting in the living room watching TV, but he muted it almost as soon as he spoke.

"Sorry 'bout that," I mumbled. "I'm going to bed. It's been a long day."

"Wait, we need to talk."

"About?"

"Come sit down," he demanded in a way that told me it was

not a request.

When Mom had gotten sick, our way of life had had to adjust. And when she had died five years ago, our life had never been the same. It was just the two of us, and I had to grow up quick. He worked swing shifts at the plant in the next town over, so I had to learn early on to take care of myself. I had been paying the bills, doing the grocery shopping, and everything else to help out since before I could drive.

Dad knew I worked hard and stayed out of trouble, but the times when he was pissed, it was obvious.

"Care to tell me about this?" he asked gruffly, reaching for my laptop that was sitting on the coffee table in front of him. He slowly opened it and turned the screen to face me.

"What are you doing with my computer?" I asked, snatching the laptop from the table.

"My house, Milo," he said. "I can do whatever I want."

"I bought this with my own money," I argued, standing up to leave the room.

"Sit back down," he insisted. "You need to explain."

"What does it matter?" I asked.

I stood up and I walked into the kitchen, clutching my laptop so tightly my knuckles were turning white. Fury carried me every step until I set the device on the table. I could hear Dad's angry steps approaching. It wasn't a habit to disrespect my dad, but he was in the wrong—not me.

"You were accepted," he said with pride in his voice. "Why didn't you tell me?"

"It's no big deal."

"The hell it isn't, Mi. This is great. I didn't even know you wanted to go to college."

He patted me on the back and smiled, but I moved away. I had been accepted two months earlier, and why I held on to the email for as long as I had was anyone's guess.

"I don't."

"Then why did you apply? And why was the acceptance email

front and center of your screen?"

"I just wanted to see if I'd get in," I admitted.

"But you don't want to go?" he asked, more to himself, like he was seeing if my words made sense.

I looked at that email almost every single day. The words that it contained haunted me.

Dear Milo,

Congratulations! It is with great pleasure that I announce your admission to Westview University.

I pulled out a chair from the table and sat down, folding my arms as I braced myself for the inevitable lecture. Dad moved to the other side and took a seat across from me. It was hard to tell what he was thinking, but that was always the case with him.

"Why didn't you accept, son?"

I raised my head and looked up at him to see if he was serious. A million reasons ran through my mind as to why I had not accepted, but it all boiled down to one thing: we could not afford it.

"I thought it would be best if I stayed here for a year. I could take some classes at CU and work at the country club. They talked about maybe giving me more responsibilities."

"But Milo…"

"Dad. I don't want to talk about it."

"And you think I'm just going to drop the subject?"

"No…but I'm hoping," I answered.

"All right, we'll circle back to that. So why don't you tell me about the girl?"

"What girl?"

"The one you got all dressed up for. Son, I know I'm not around much, but I do know things."

He smiled knowingly and waited for me to offer more, but there was not anything to share. Not yet, anyway. Our entire evening had revolved around Meg and her leaving. We didn't have much time alone, except for the drive to and from the party. Our conversation had flowed much easier than it ever had before, but we had never managed to talk about our earlier conversation.

"Her name is Holland. We work together."

"And?"

"And? We went to her friend's going away party—that's it."

"But you want more."

"Wanting and getting are two different things. You know that better than anyone."

Dad's eyes turned sad when he looked at me, and I felt like a jerk. I was not trying to sound so cruel, but I had learned early on that not everything works out the way we want. Case in point: *Mom.*

When she was dying, Mom had told me the story about how she had met Dad. It was spun as the old-fashioned, boy-meets-girl trope. But when Dad left the hospital room and it was just the two of us, she had told me the real story.

My dad did not have an easy life. He came from an abusive home where he bore the brunt of the abuse to protect his mom and sister. At the time, Mom was engaged to someone else and she had just graduated from high school. According to Mom, the guy was stable, smart, popular—and boring to a fault. As I recalled, she said he was so dull it was hard for her to stay awake when they tried to have conversations. Still, he was the obvious choice because of where he came from and who he was.

But that changed when she was at a diner having breakfast alone. Dad walked in and sat at the table next to hers, a disheveled mess. According to Mom, she had seen him before because they went to the same church, so she knew of him. But that morning at the diner, that was the first time she *really* noticed him.

"He was a mess," she said with a smile.

Her frail hand patted mine and she looked up as she recalled the memory like it was happening in front of her right then.

"He had a cut just over his right eye and his lip was swollen. If your grandmother would have seen him that morning, there's no way she would've let me speak to him, let alone date him."

"So what happened?" I asked, because I wanted to hear her talk more. The sound of her voice calmed the frightened kid who knew he had little time left with the most important woman in his life.

"I talked to him," she said. "He was quiet and shy, but so handsome."

"Even with the cut and busted lip?"

"I saw through all of that. I saw him," she answered. "Oh don't get me wrong—we haven't had a fairytale romance. No relationship is like they show in movies, honey. But your father is the most gentle, loving, caring, strong man that I know. He had a hard time letting me in."

"Why?"

"Because, he was afraid to be happy. He'd spent his whole life being told he wasn't good enough, smart enough, strong enough—so to have me come in and love him, despite all he'd been taught to believe, it scared him. Hope wasn't something he believed in."

"So why are you telling me this now?"

She took a deep breath—those had become hard for her—and cleared her throat before speaking. There were tears in her eyes and she squeezed my hand tightly.

"Because, honey, he deserved all the wonderful things that we've shared together—and I'm not going to be around to make sure that you know that for yourself."

"I'm sorry," I said to Dad as I ran my hand through my hair. "I didn't mean that."

"Yes you did—and maybe it's time we have a talk."

"There's nothing to talk about. I mean, I thought that maybe we'd get to talk tonight, but that didn't exactly work out."

"Milo, you have this defeatist attitude about everything. Maybe I should have done more for you when your mom died—reassured you that everything would be okay."

"It's fine."

"No. Let me speak," he demanded.

Dad remained quiet and looked down at his hands. He still wore his wedding ring, and pictures of Mom were strategically placed in the areas of the home where she had spent most of her time. He had never moved on, and some days I thought he believed that she wasn't really gone. We never talked about it because it was too hard for either of us.

"Somewhere between Mom getting sick and her dying, you stopped believing in anything good. You stopped hoping. I saw it happening before my eyes, but I was so consumed in my own grief that I didn't help you—and that was selfish of me."

"Dad, it was bad for both of us. You can't beat yourself up about that."

"Maybe not, and maybe that excuse was okay for the first year, but it's been five. You're so much like your mom. You got your brain and your talent from her, no doubt about that."

"What are you trying to say?"

He sighed and looked at me with defeat that I had only seen in his eyes after she died. He had managed to pick up the pieces and dove in, headfirst, into work. I knew he missed her every single day, but he never showed it.

"Milo, your mom would be pissed at me if she knew what I let you become."

"Damn, thanks, Dad," I deadpanned.

"If she knew that you gave up on things before you even tried them, she'd kick both of our asses."

"I graduated in the top ten percent," I reminded him. "That doesn't exactly scream slacker, Dad."

"No, but you sell yourself short—you don't allow yourself to dream or believe that you deserve good things, and I think that's my fault. I didn't tell you often enough how proud I am of you, or that you should dream big."

"I know you're proud."

"If you want to go to college, you should go. If you want to pursue culinary school, you should apply. If you want the girl, you should tell her."

"It's fine. I'm fine."

"No it's not. You never mentioned college to me, and I didn't want to pressure you if that wasn't what you wanted, but clearly I was wrong. About a lot of things."

"I don't want to go to college," I argued. "I just…"

"I know, you wanted to see if you'd get in—and you did. So obviously it's something that you have at least considered."

I stood up from the table and pushed in my chair. As I passed him on the way to my room, I stopped and placed my hand on his shoulder. If he could manage it, I knew he would send me to any college I wanted. The ability to afford it was something I had come to terms with when the medical bills had started pouring in after Mom died. Hundreds of thousands of dollars to pay for specialists, tests, private rooms, and everything else to keep her with us just a little longer.

And I would have gladly stood by and watched Dad spend more, just to have another day with her.

"I don't know what my next step is, but I promise it will be something great."

"I'm gonna hold you to that, Mi. And just so you know, whatever it is you want, I will do whatever I can to make it happen."

"Thanks, Dad."

CHAPTER 7

HOLLAND

After Milo and I left Meg's party, she texted me and demanded that I stay the night. She only had two more nights at home before she would be gone for college, and I wasn't ready to say goodbye. I was more than happy to spend some quality time with the person I considered a sister.

There was so much I wanted to talk to her about, but didn't know where to start. So much of our lives were wrapped up in each other, and for the first time since we were five, we would be separated.

But instead of having one of our long nights of talking, we decided to keep it low-key. Sitting on her bed watching *Pretty in Pink*, one of our favorite movies, we were quoting it line for line. No one liked watching movies with us because we could never be quiet. In fact, we were often just plain annoying.

"So are you and Milo dating?" Meg asked nonchalantly.

"I don't think so," I said, shoving a pile of popcorn into my mouth.

"You don't think so," she repeated. "Care to explain?"

I tried to buy myself some time by grabbing another handful of popcorn, but she stopped my hand from reaching the intended target.

"Don't avoid the question."

I rolled my eyes and opened my hand, dropping the fluffy popcorn back into the bowl. She kept her mouth shut and avoided saying anything else. I knew she would remain quiet until I gave her what she wanted.

"He asked me out today."

"Really? And? Are you going?"

"No, I mean, he asked me to go out—today. But I declined so I could come to your party. And granted, he came with me, but after he dropped me off at home, he didn't ask me out again…I mean, we stood there all quiet and weird and he had more than enough time to make a move."

"So you wanted him to do something," she surmised.

"Yeah…I guess I did. Before, he put it all out there and made it sound like he was interested in me. But then nothing."

"Give him some time. After all this time, he finally got up the nerve to ask you out. Maybe he thought you rejected him."

"Great…If that's the case, work is going to be awkward tomorrow," I teased.

Our attention was back on the movie because she knew it was my favorite scene. Duckie was the perfect guy, making a fool of himself just for the girl he loved.

"Why is she so stupid?" I asked, pointing at Molly Ringwald's character.

Meg looked at me and gave me a lopsided grin. It was something we always debated, and of course the movie always ended the same. Still, for some crazy reason I held out hope that she would choose the right guy. I was watching him dance all over the record store when my phone buzzed in my hand. I figured my parents were probably checking in, so I was surprised that it was actually Milo texting me. I felt my smile grow as I responded, happy that he wanted to see me again. Of course I decided to play dumb and asked if he meant another party.

I started laughing nervously and Meg paused the movie and snatched the phone from my hand so she could read it. I didn't care that she was looking at it because I was going to show her anyway. Her smile was wide and her eyes crinkled at the sides when she looked at me.

"You two are so cute," she gushed.

She didn't give me a chance to say anything because she started typing out something on my phone. When I tried to grab it from her, she pushed her elbow out toward me to keep me from taking it away from her.

"Sent," she said proudly, finally handing my phone back to me.

"What did you do?" I asked before looking at the screen.

Me (really Meg): Can't wait. Let me know when and I'll be there.

"Jeez, Meg! You made me sound desperate," I said, setting my phone down on her nightstand.

"No. I made you sound interested...which you are. So you're welcome."

"Since when did you become the brazen one?"

"When I realized I only have one more day before I'm gone and swimming in a bigger pond. Gotta put myself out there."

"You mean you have to put *me* out there."

"Same thing. I have another date with Knox tomorrow before I leave."

"Look at you, growing up," I gushed.

Meg smiled and looked so proud of herself for the next step she was about to take. I was proud of her, too. For years, Meg was the one who went with the flow, worked her ass off for her grades, and got into her dream college. For all the leaps of faith she took for her future, her present was what had concerned me. She had missed out on all the dating, the parties, the high school experience. Sure, she would go with me from time to time, but the bottom line was that Meg had a plan, and she was not about to risk it for anything stupid like one crazy night out.

And she had earned her spot. For that, I could not have been more proud. Or more sad. She was about to leave me, and despite how much we wanted to pretend like things would always be the same between us, deep down we knew what was likely to happen.

"You're going to own that pond," I told her, fighting back my tears.

"You think?"

"I know it. You've got this."

Meg smiled, her eyes rimmed red with unshed tears. "Yeah I do."

"And I can't wait to hear all about it."

"You know you're the first one I'll tell."

"I know."

When her smile began to fade, she looked around her room and sighed. We had been friends since we were five years old, and in all that time, the room had barely changed. She had most of her clothes packed into moving boxes stacked in the corner of her room, but the walls were still lined with old pictures and decorations that indicated a preteen, not the college student about to leave.

"Having second thoughts?" I asked playfully.

"About college? No. About everything else...yeah."

"What do you mean?"

"High school, I guess. When I come back, will people even remember me because I wasn't around much?"

I grabbed Meg's hand and squeezed it until she looked at me. When she did, I smiled as the first tear began to fall.

"I'll remember you. For the rest of my life, you will be my first and best friend and there will never be another who could hold a candle to you. Screw everyone else and whether or not they remember you, because the important people will. Who cares if you didn't party or date every guy who looked your way? What matters is who you are. Those of us lucky enough to know you, *know you*, Meg and what a wonderful person you are. Trust me, we won't forget."

Meg wiped her eyes with her free hand before pulling me into a tight hug. We clung to each other as our tears fell, both sad to let go and excited about what was to come.

"This isn't how I wanted to spend tonight," she said through a sniffle.

I laughed and pulled away, wiping my eyes as I looked at her. "No? You didn't want to cry until your head hurt, get puffy eyes, and probably a headache?" I laughed.

"Now, while that all sounds amazing…no."

"All right, this is your shindig—what's the plan?"

"Movies, junk food, and no sleep."

"Movies and junk food, count me in. But sleep…I have to work tomorrow."

"Afternoon. You work tomorrow afternoon."

"Fine, but if I look like a mess at work, I'm blaming you."

"I'm sure Milo won't mind," she teased.

***

It was nearly two in the morning when Meg finally fell asleep. She was always the first one to crash, but usually it was eleven or so. Knowing that this was my last night in her room, the last sleepover as kids, it was hard for me to close my eyes.

I started looking through my phone when I noticed that I had another text from Milo, that he had sent earlier. Reluctantly I opened the message and saw there were actually three texts from him.

Milo: Tomorrow? After work?

I reread the text that Meg sent for me and realized that he was asking me out, and I never responded. I looked at the next text, one he sent an hour later.

Milo: Or whenever. It's cool.

Milo: OK. Guess I'll see you at work tomorrow.

Before I could talk myself out of it, I typed out a message that I could go out after work, hopeful that he was still interested. Three little dots appeared and I smiled.

Milo: What are you doing awake?

Me: What are you doing awake?

Milo: I asked you first

Me: Meg wanted to stay up all night. Sorry I didn't see your text.

Milo: It's fine.

Me: You didn't tell me why you're awake

The three dots seemed to blink for an eternity and then they disappeared, only to blink again. I figured he was typing some long explanation, and then his text came through.

Milo: I was waiting for you

My stomach swirled nervously, and there was no reason to even try to contain my smile. This guy, who I had wanted to just acknowledge my existence, was flirting with me. And I liked it.

Me: Why?

Milo: Why not?

Me: You're different in text. Is this really Milo?

I smiled and waited for his response. Milo was never talkative in class, at least not around me. But he had talked to everyone at the party. He was smiling and engaging, until I was around. He seemed to quiet in my presence, and I was sort of jealous that I had not gotten to engage with the other version of him. But when we were texting, he seemed to open up.

> *Milo: It's me. I guess this is just easier.*
> *Me: Okay, then perhaps I should use this to my advantage.*
> *Milo: How so?*
> *Me: Get you to tell me some things.*
> *Milo: Like?*
> *Me: Why didn't you talk to me at school?*
> *Milo: I already told you.*

When we had talked at work, he admitted that he liked me. Still, that seemed unlikely considering he had never taken the time to get to know me. What was it about me that he liked so much?

> *Me: You said that you liked me - but how do you know that?*
> *Milo: How do I know I like you?*
> *Me: Yeah, because you don't even really know me.*
> *Milo: I know you, Holland. Your smile is infectious. You're smart and kind. You're beautiful. And when you think no one is looking, you let your guard down and I see your insecurities. You wonder if you're good enough, or smart enough, or pretty enough. But you weren't always like that.*

How could he see all of that? I wanted to argue to tell him he was absolutely wrong about that last part, but it was true. The last year of school had tested the positive outlook I had on my future, and that was something I had not bothered to share, even with Meg.

> *Me: How do you know all of this?*

64

Milo: Because I see you.

Me: I wish you would have talked to me in school.

Milo: Well, you make me nervous

Me: You make me nervous, too

Milo: Why?

Me: Because you're so quiet and intense

Milo: Intense?

Me: Did you read what you just texted me? That's pretty intense.

Milo: I'm sorry. I didn't mean to scare you.

Me: It's not that. I'm just confused because the way you looked at me, I always thought you were judging me

Milo: No. I just couldn't take my eyes off you

I was glad Meg had fallen asleep, because she could read me better than anyone, and if she saw my face she'd know that Milo was saying all the right things. Or at least texting them.

Me: Is text the only way I'll know how you feel or what you're thinking?

Milo: Depends. Can I take you out tomorrow?

Me: Yes. If you can promise me one thing.

Milo: What's that?

Me: We can talk more about this.

Milo: Okay.

Me: Okay.

Milo: Goodnight Holland.

Me: Goodnight.

CHAPTER 8

MILO

Sleep was the furthest thing from my mind after the talk with Dad about college. All I could do was stare at the email,—the one that would have changed the trajectory of my future…a future that was too far out of my reach. I thought about what my mom would want for me and I knew she would be on the same page as my dad. Of course they wanted me to be happy, in whatever form that was. College was not something I talked about often; in fact, Ethan was the only one who knew I had applied anywhere. Going away and getting an engineering degree was what I wanted more than I would admit.

But I did not want my dad to feel bad about not being able to afford to send me to college. I had known for some time that it just was not in the cards for me, and somewhere along the way, I had accepted it. But that didn't mean I didn't want to know for myself if I *could* do it.

My counselor had talked to me at the beginning of senior year about my plans. She threw out words like *financial aid*, *student loans*, and *scholarships* as if I had not heard of them. I knew those were options, but setting myself up for disappointment—or worse, a life of debt—was not.

Luckily, my evening took a turn for the better and the thoughts about my future were momentarily out of my thoughts. I was lying in bed, staring up at the ceiling, debating what I really wanted when my phone screen lit up next to my bedside. I reached over and picked it up, noticing it was after three in the morning. Holland's name was there in front of me and I opened the text, happy to hear from her.

If I did not want to face the realities of college, I could think about her and how much I enjoyed being with her. I still found myself somewhat tongue-tied around her, but at least we were hanging out with other people I knew. And with the added push from Meg, I had decided that I would reach out. I was surprised when she was so eager to go out, but as soon as I named a time and a place, she went silent.

Maybe she had second thoughts, or maybe she had other things going on and could not respond. Needless to say, I glad she was texting me, even if it was incredibly late. And while it was not for very long, what we wrote to each other felt more serious than the few conversations we had had up to that point.

I hated that it was so hard for me to talk to her. But in text— maybe it was because I wasn't looking into those light brown eyes that made me lose all rational thoughts—I was able to be honest with her. And because she had asked me to, I would try to make more of an effort when I saw her again.

Unfortunately, when our shift at work rolled around that afternoon, we barely had a chance to say hello. Carlo's special brought so many patrons into the restaurant that the waiting list was easily an hour. Most of the staff barely had a moment to take a break because the demand was nonstop.

"That girl is hot," Brandon said, leaning against the counter as I prepped the vegetables for Carlo.

"What?" I asked as I slid a tray over so Jaysen could take it to the chef.

"Holland," Brandon said, and I felt my pulse begin to tick

faster. "The new girl."

"I know who she is," I grumbled.

Brandon had not seemed to notice or care that I had no interest in what he was saying—not that he ever really cared. He loved to hear himself talk and thought everyone else felt the same way. He failed to realize that most of the people in the kitchen tolerated him because he was a good waiter and the ladies who came to the restaurant seemed to like him. The staff thought of him as a douchebag. And I never considered him at all because he never bothered me.

Until he talked about Holland.

"Oh yeah, y'all went to school together, right?"

"Yeah."

I busied myself with the next prep, but Brandon just kept on talking. I was not sure what I was doing that made him think I was listening to him, or maybe he just didn't care.

"Don't you have tables?" I asked.

He waved off my question and shrugged.

"Listen, do me a favor and see if she's dating anyone."

"No thanks."

"C'mon. Just talk to her for me."

I set my knife on the counter louder than necessary, which caused both Carlo and Jaysen to stop what they were doing. The head chef looked over to see what was going on, but kept quiet for a moment before speaking.

"You good?" Carlo asked with his usual even tone.

"Yeah. Just realized I forgot to start simmering the sauce," I lied.

"You need to take care of that," Carlo snapped.

Brandon was not one to respond to many people in the kitchen, but hearing the tone in the chef's voice, he hurried off to take care of his tables. And when he was out of earshot, Carlo looked at me and gave me a nod. I appreciated that he had maintained my lie, because that evening's special didn't call for a sauce.

I wanted to shut Brandon's thoughts of Holland down as soon as he started talking about her. I wanted to tell him that she was going out with me after work, but it wasn't my place. While I felt territorial of her, she wasn't mine. She did not belong to me or anyone else, and if she decided that she was interested in him, unfortunately there was not much I could do about that.

The one thing I did know, ever since she had agreed to go out with me, I felt like at least one thing was going my way.

"You should take a break," Jaysen said when he stood next to me.

I looked down at the food I still needed to work up, but he just stepped into my space, basically pushing me out of the way.

"I'm good," I said, reaching for the vegetables.

"No. You need to take a break," he repeated.

He cleared his throat and tilted his head toward the back door. I noticed that it had closed and I wasn't sure why there was a need for me to take a break. I was about to insist on continuing my work when he widened his eyes.

"All right. I'll go."

I tossed my towel onto the counter and walked toward the exit, still confused. The warm afternoon air hit me with a stifling suffocation. It was barely June, but it might as well have been August because the humidity felt like one hundred percent.

"Are you following me?" I heard her voice ask before I saw her.

I looked to the right, behind the door, and saw Holland sitting on the bench scrolling through her phone. Her hair was pulled into her usual ponytail, with a few curls that seemed to have escaped its grasp. I recalled our text from the night before and knew that I had to do better with communicating with her in person. I wanted her to know how I felt about her without hiding behind a screen. It was out of my comfort zone, but she had asked me to try.

"Not intentionally," I said as I walked toward her. "Mind if I sit with you?"

"Sure." She smiled, scooting over to make room for me.

She put her phone away inside of her apron and turned toward me. I never tired of looking at her, but I guess the way I stared was off-putting.

"Busy night."

"Yeah. What's that about?" she asked.

"Carlo. His slow-roasted garlic pork is a huge hit. It used to be featured weekly, but we couldn't keep up with the demand. Hendricks decided to do it once a month. Hence the insane crowd."

"Yeah, I thought it was strange that so many people would show up this early. Sounds like I need to give this dish a try," she said with a smirk.

"I'm sure I can arrange that."

She bit her lip as her smile began to grow. I loved that I could make her face light up the way it did with just that simple promise.

"Any plans tonight?" I asked.

She narrowed her eyes playfully and grinned. "Yeah, I've got a date."

"Anyone I know?"

"Just someone I went to school with."

"That's cool," I said, feigning disinterest.

"What about you?" she asked, playing along.

"Well, I was going to ask you out, but if you already have plans…"

"I suppose I could get out of them," she answered quickly. "That is, if you're asking me out."

"Don't you think he'll be disappointed if you canceled?"

Holland shrugged. "Not sure. He's never talked to me very much."

"Sounds like a jerk."

A small sound of laughter escaped her and I immediately loved the sound. I made a mental note right then to make her laugh as often as I could. If her smile lit up a room, her laugh kept it

70

going.

"I don't think he's a jerk...but I reserve the right to decide that once I actually get to know him."

"That's really fair of you."

"I like to try to keep an open mind."

I wanted to kiss her. I knew it was irrational, and not the right time, but I wanted to hold her. The silence settled between us, and just as I was about to speak, the back door swung open.

"There you are," Brandon said gruffly. "Daphne is looking for you."

"Thanks," she said, hopping to her feet.

Brandon let the door slam shut behind him when he walked inside, and Holland rolled her eyes. If she knew he was interested in her, she didn't show it, or show any interest in return. She started walking inside but stopped and looked back at me.

"You are still taking me out, right?" she asked.

"Absolutely."

She smiled and went inside without another word, leaving me alone on the bench. It was the most we had spoken, which was sad, given that I had gone to Meg's party with her. I felt like the invitation was a pity invite, and every time we were around each other, it was awkward silences and strained conversation. This time it was playful, and I had allowed myself to flirt with her. And Holland had seemed to enjoy it as much as I did.

Our shifts would not be done until five, and I knew that I wanted to make our first date special. Though I was not sure how I would accomplish that, I had a few ideas I had come up with while trying to go to sleep after the party.

"We need you inside," Jaysen said when he opened the door.

I stood up and walked inside, and thanked him for sending me out to Holland.

"Brandon walked back inside bragging that you were talking him up to her," he laughed. "Jackass."

"Yeah? Well, I can say his name never came up."

"Figured, since you're obviously into her."

Just as I opened my mouth to protest, Jaysen shook his head and scoffed.

"Does everyone know?" I asked.

"Nah. But you better make a move before he decides to ask her out."

"He can ask all he wants to, but she's going out with me tonight."

Jaysen patted my back proudly and grinned. "Tonight? Good for you."

"Yeah...Hey, maybe you can help me?"

"Whatcha need?"

"Food. I was telling her about the special."

"Say no more. I got ya covered."

"Thanks, man. Appreciate it."

"No worries. But get back to work before Carlo kills both of us. And if he asks, you had a family issue to deal with, all right?"

"Got it."

"Any idea where you're taking her?"

Several places came to mind, but there was one place where I knew we would be able to talk and hang out without interruption.

CHAPTER 9

HOLLAND

"Milo, this is incredible," I said, savoring another bite of Carlo's special from the restaurant.

"Told you it's good."

"No, I believe the word is 'amazing.' No wonder people wait for this."

When Milo had found me outside taking a break at work, I was nervous to see him after our texts. I liked the guy I was texting, but he was different from the guy I had known in school. He really took my request to heart and made an effort to talk to me—and albeit an odd interaction, it was flirtatious and made me smile. The banter about *someone* taking me out made me laugh, and I loved that he played along. And then Brandon had to walk outside and interrupt us.

"I'm so full." I laughed, pushing thoughts of Brandon and his bad timing out of my mind as I patted my stomach. "I could fall asleep right here."

"Considering how late you stayed up, I'm sure you could."

"What time did you go to bed?"

"I'm not really sure."

"So you're tired, too."

He smiled at me and shook his head. "But if you want to go home, I won't be offended."

"No," I said a little too eagerly. "I don't want to go home."

"Can I show you something?" he asked.

"Okay."

Milo stood up from the picnic table and placed all containers inside the plastic bag that he brought with him. I wiped my hands off on a paper napkin before wadding it up and tossing it into the trash. The sun was beginning to set and the heat was not as bad as it had been earlier that day. We walked toward the playground side by side in comfortable silence.

He could have taken me to any number of places for our date, but he had picked one of my absolute favorite spots. Jenkins Memorial Park was the one place Meg and I spent our summers when we were kids. Nearly every day of our break was spent running around the slides and swings. The city had upgraded the playground equipment, but for the most part, it was still the same.

"What made you want to bring me here?" I asked.

He smiled. "You'll see."

I knew every inch of the park. There was not a single place that Meg and I had not explored as kids, so I was curious what was so secret.

As we walked, his arm brushed against mine and I felt the tingles that traveled up my arm. Butterflies and tingles made first dates and new relationships so exciting...not that it was anything more than a date. I was getting ahead of myself, thinking about being close to Milo when he could very easily decide that he didn't like me after all.

I swallowed hard, feeling nervous and excited at the same time. I really wanted to feel that jolt again to see if it was just a fluke, to see if I was creating it all in my head. But then he reached down between us and his hand found mine. It felt timid and hopeful—or maybe that was just me. And then he threaded his fingers with mine, squeezing gently.

When I looked up at him, as if sensing my own questions, he looked down at me and smiled. I felt my heart beat faster in my chest and knew right then that I was blushing. This guy, this kind and quiet enigma who I had thought hated me, had changed everything in just a few short days. He made me question my perception of every interaction we had ever had.

We stopped walking when we reached a bench that was sat between two weeping willows that overlooked the pond. On the other side of the water was Pine Bridge Forest, a protected area that would, fortunately, never be developed.

"I love it out here," I said as we took a seat.

"My mom used to bring me out here…before she got sick."

I remembered the news of his mom dying and how sad he had looked when he came back to school. I had never lost anyone that close to me and I couldn't imagine how hard that would be, especially at such a young age.

"What else did she do with you?" I asked as I stared into the distance.

"She sang. All the time. I don't think there was a single day where she wasn't singing."

"Did you sing too?"

Milo laughed and shook his head. "I guess I have an okay voice, but nothing like her. When I was a kid, she would sing some funny song to wake me up in the morning…and she sang me to sleep every night. Mom was always smiling and doing her best to make everyone around her happy."

"She sounds perfect."

"Well, she was just about perfect…except for one thing."

"What's that?" I asked.

"She was a terrible cook," he said with a laugh. "I mean, just awful. She burned water!"

"How do you burn water?" I asked.

Milo just chuckled and kept talking. "I went in and asked if I could help. I was old enough to follow directions in a book. I think she was just happy that I wanted to be with her. But then I sort of took over. Mom got me everything I needed, and before we knew it, we'd cooked chicken marsala."

"Wow. Impressive. And you were how old?"

He looked down at me as he tried to recall his age. I wanted to look away because he made me nervous, but I didn't. Instead, I patiently waited while he thought, and stared into those brown eyes.

"I guess I was about ten or so."

"So she's the reason you like cooking?"

"Yeah, I guess so."

"Is that what you're going to study in college?"

Milo sat up a little straighter, forcing me to adjust my spot next to him. There was a small space between us and I wished that I was once again close enough to touch him.

"Doesn't Meg leave today?" he asked.

The familiar sadness of her going away filled me again. When I had left her house that morning, I knew it would be the last time I would see her for a while. One of the reasons I had agreed to the date with Milo was for the distraction, but there it was: the truth that my best friend would be gone.

"I'm sorry…I didn't mean to upset you."

"No. I'm fine. Or I will be."

"You two really are close, huh?"

"I can't tell her, but I'm so sad that she's leaving. I'm scared that once she goes away, everything will be different."

"Different isn't always a bad thing."

"True."

"And it's not like you won't talk to her anymore," he said with a smile.

"I'm expecting a call from her later tonight."

"When she gets to Stedham?"

"Yes…and no. She had a date with Knox before she left town," I laughed. "Never in a million years did I think Meg and

Knox would go on a date."

"Well, I bet you never thought you'd be out with me either."

"You got me there."

It was the perfect moment for him to kiss me. He made being with him so easy, and I wanted to know if what I was feeling was all a fantasy I was making up. Because at that moment, I could see myself spending all of my free time with him. After one date, Milo had made me realize that he was what I wanted. But there was no kiss, just his hand finding mine once more. As we sat on the bench, our fingers entwined, the quiet began to stretch.

Our moment had passed.

We watched the sun dip low behind the trees as the warm summer air swirled around us. I was beyond tired, but I was not ready for him to take me home yet.

"You realize this can't go anywhere," Milo said so quietly that I thought maybe I had imagined it.

"What's that?" I asked, hoping he was not talking about whatever it was that was happening between us.

"You and me."

My heart sank, which seemed odd because what did I know about Milo except the few details I had learned over the span of few days? But I missed him already, and I didn't know why.

Milo gently nudged my arm with his and waited for me to look at him. Slowly I turned my head to the side and was faced with those brown eyes that had always made me feel judged. But all I saw was the disappointment that I felt reflected in his eyes. I nodded once and offered a sad smile as I started to look away. He had just broken up with me and we were not even together.

Why did that hurt?

He held my hand a little tighter and I squeezed back only to feel his free hand graze my chin, pulling me to look at him.

"I know," I said.

Milo was as frustrated by his words as I was, and I could tell by his heavy sigh. As I started to pull away, I looked at him and found a defiance building inside me that had me shaking my head.

Before I could talk myself out of it or rationalize why he was right, I leaned forward and pressed my lips to his, catching him off guard.

It only took a moment for him to wrap his arms around me, pulling me close against him. My hand was resting against his chest while he trailed a hand up to my neck, holding me gently. Our mouths melded to each other's and I knew I had never felt a kiss so perfectly. When we parted, I closed my eyes as I tried to hold on to that feeling a little longer. His forehead was rested against mine and I realized Milo must have felt the same way because he had not moved away from me.

"You shouldn't have done that," he whispered.

"Why?"

"Because now I have to take back everything I just said."

"Which part?"

"This is going somewhere. I'm just not sure I'll be okay when it's over."

"Me either," said quietly.

The truth of that admission hit me hard, and I knew that when it was time to leave for college, there was a chance it would be the hardest thing I would have to do.

"So what do we do?" I asked. "Given the inevitable?"

"I guess make the most of it."

"And how would you suggest we do that?"

He kissed me again quickly and stood up, pulling me to my feet. I happily followed as he held my hand and brought me to the edge of the water.

"What? Are you going to push me in?" I asked as I looked at him.

He pretended to consider it for a moment and then smiled. "No. Of course not. But…"

"No way!" I laughed, taking a step back.

"I'm kidding. But we'll just spend as much time together as we can."

"I can do that. I'm sure my family will be okay with me disappearing from time to time so we can go to dinner or see a movie."

"I'm thinking something different. Not crazy different, but definitely not the same lame dinner-and-movie dates."

"What? Skydiving?" I laughed, but when I looked at him, his eyes were wide and his smile grew. "No. No way! I don't jump out of perfectly good planes."

"Aw c'mon, isn't that on your bucket list?"

"Yeah, right up there with climbing Mount Everest."

"Okay, so maybe not that crazy, but what if we made a list of things we want to do together before you—we—leave for school?"

"So like a date bucket list?" I asked.

"Sure."

"I think I could get on board with that."

***

When I got home that night, Mom and Dad were sitting outside enjoying a glass of wine and talking. It had become a nightly routine for them to sit and talk before going to bed, and I didn't want to interrupt them.

"How was work?" Mom asked.

"Busy. But I made some great tips, so that's good."

"I'm proud of you, Hollz," Dad said. "You could spend your summer working on your tan and doing nothing, but you're getting out there and keeping yourself busy."

"Thanks, Dad."

"How was your date?" Mom asked with a cheeky grin. "It was a date, right?"

I could not help but smile thinking about Milo. When he dropped me off, he had wanted to walk me up to the door, and there he had kissed me for the millionth time that night.

"It was nice."

"Where did y'all go?" Dad asked.

"He took me on a picnic to Jenkins."

"Definitely a great night to be outside," Mom said. "Did he make dinner?"

"Sort of. He got us a couple of the specials from earlier. It was awesome," I gushed.

"I don't want to rain on your parade," Dad started, "but is it wise to start seeing someone from home just before you leave for college?"

"Is it wise? I doubt it. Is my heart going to break when it's over? Probably. Am I doing it anyway? Hell yeah," I said without hesitation.

Dad nodded and grinned at my mom. "Sounds good."

"I'm going to text Meg. Love you both," I said before walking back inside the house.

I walked into my room and closed the door behind me. I looked at my reflection in the mirror and noticed the smile of the woman who stood in front of me. Things with Blake had ended badly and I didn't care to get back out on the dating scene, but I was glad that Milo had asked me out. And I was equally glad I had agreed to go out with him.

He surpassed any expectations I had, and his date idea had me more excited than I had thought possible.

Me: You busy?

Meg: Just studying. What's up?

I started to think of everything that had happened with Milo—the flirting, the kiss, the almost pre-dating breakup—and I knew it was too much to text.

Me: Can you talk?

She didn't respond, and soon my phone lit up with her name. I answered it on the first ring, so happy to hear her voice.

"How's the new dorm?"

"It's overwhelming," she sighed. "I'll only admit that to you, because Mom and Dad will worry if I tell them it's anything less than perfect."

"Are they staying at a hotel or something?"

"Yeah, I think they're staying through the weekend to make sure I'm okay," she laughed.

"And are you okay?"

"Yes and no," she admitted. "I'm really nervous."

"I know you're going to be great."

"Thanks…but it's nice to be able to say that out loud to someone else."

"That's what I'm here for. No need for perfection and pretenses with me."

"And that's why I love you," she said.

"Have you met your roommate?"

"Not yet. She gets in tomorrow, I think," Meg said. "Keep your fingers crossed we get along."

"I'm sure it'll be great."

"So what's up?" she asked.

"I had a date," I said eagerly.

I heard her squeal on the other end of the line and started laughing. When we had said our goodbyes before she left the day before, she had urged me to be open to the possibilities with Milo. Not all guys are users and jerks like Blake, and while I knew that, it was still nice to hear.

"How was it?"

"Great. Until he broke up with me," I laughed.

"He broke up with you? I didn't realize one date counts as a relationship," she teased.

"He didn't want to risk us getting hurt when it came time for college."

She was quiet for a second and I wondered if she had heard

what I said. I could always count on Meg to give it to me straight, even when I was sure I did *not* want to hear it.

"I guess I understand…but…wait, you sound too happy. Either you were relieved or you changed his mind."

"I kissed him," I said proudly. "I told him no—we're going to do this."

"Well look at you, all assertive," she said.

"I'm always assertive," I reminded her.

"Yeah. I know."

"I have a feeling that when this is over, I'm going to be crushed…and oddly, I'm okay with that."

"At least you know what you're getting into."

"Okay, changing the subject back to you—how was your lunch date with Knox?"

Meg sighed happily and I could picture her dreamy smile as she thought of him.

"Perfect. And awful."

"Explain."

"I'm just sort of beating myself up for not stepping out of my shell sooner. For not talking to him. I was so scared to embarrass myself that I didn't really put myself out there. With anyone. Ever! But we had so much fun together. And when he kissed me…"

"He kissed you?"

"Yes. When he dropped me back off at home. I know that it's over before it even got started, and I sort of wish I was staying home for the summer to see how it all played out. Probably would have ended with me crying and not wanting to leave, so maybe it's for the best."

The scenario played out in my head, only it wasn't Knox and Meg—it was Milo and me. It would only end one way, and if I thought about the bad side of it, I knew I would talk myself out of experiencing the good.

"But maybe it'll be different for you and Milo," she said when she realized what she had said.

"It's fine," I told her. "That's the reason he didn't want to date. But I think I'll hate myself if I don't give it a chance. I really like him, Meg. He's so sweet and funny…"

"And he's not bad on the eyes either," she teased.

"Yeah, there's that too. But there's just something about the way he looks at me. I wish he'd told me sooner how he felt about me. Maybe I would have avoided the whole Blake thing."

"But what do I always tell you?"

I rolled my eyes and knew she wouldn't say a word until I said what she wanted to hear. "Everything happens for a reason."

"And maybe the reason is so you could spot a great guy in a sea of jackasses."

"I like that," I laughed. "It makes sense."

"Of course it does, because I'm a genius."

"You're cocky, is what you are. What happened to Meg?" I laughed.

"She was kissed by Knox. She's a cocky bitch now," she deadpanned.

My phone vibrated against my ear and I pulled it away to see a text from Milo.

Milo: When is your next day off?

Me: Sunday

Milo: I work in the morning. Can I take you out?

Me: Yes

Milo: Hope you have a bathing suit and water shoes

Me: Where are we going?

Milo:

Me: hello? Where are we going?

"Hello?" Meg asked. "Are you still there?"

"Sorry! Milo texted."

"He misses you already?"

"He wants to take me out Sunday. He said I need a bathing suit."

"What's the mystery? You're going swimming."

"Well, not exactly. We're sort of each coming up with a list of fun, different, memorable dates, and then we're doing those."

"I love it. But wait, how is swimming something memorable?"

"I have no idea."

"Well, this should be fun," she laughed.

CHAPTER 10

HOLLAND

I never kept secrets from Meg. She was the one person who knew everything about me and loved me anyway. We had told each other so many secrets that not having each other in our lives would be a very stupid move on either of our parts. When we were kids, we had even decided to go the route of being blood sisters, but got squeamish when it came to actually drawing blood. I think we both knew then that there was nothing that would keep us apart. Even distance.

We got off the phone and set an appointment in our calendars to talk every Wednesday night, no matter what. If we talked on other days, it didn't matter—we had a standing date.

And she was the only person who knew about Milo and me. Sure, Mom and Dad knew about the date, and while I wanted everyone to know about us, I didn't know his thoughts. I knew little about Milo, but I was certain of his desire for privacy and I wanted to be respectful of that.

"Hey," I said as I walked past Milo, adjusting my apron.

"Hey," he answered, and I turned around.

He was looking at me with a shy smile that made my stomach flip excitedly. My eyes caught sight of his forearms, where his shirt was rolled up, as they flexed while he worked. Things about Milo I had never noticed before became fixations. His hands, his arms, the vein in his neck that pulsed when he was nervous—all of them were things I seemed to focus on.

Milo and I were scheduled to get off work at the same time Saturday afternoon. I had noticed it when I looked to see what days I would work the next week. We decided that we would hang out for a little, but our mystery date was still set for Sunday. With a beautiful day at my disposal, I was glad I had brought my bathing suit with me so I could lay out after my shift. It had been a long afternoon and I was looking forward to enjoying the clear summer day.

I walked out to the restaurant to find Brandon carrying a tray to one of my tables. I hurried over to take over so my customers didn't think I had forgotten about them.

"Thanks," I whispered to Brandon.

"No problem," he said with a smirk. "Anytime."

I made quick time of setting the plates in front of the patrons before checking if they needed anything else. Once I was back in the kitchen, I placed the empty tray on the counter inside the kitchen and sighed. It had been a particularly busy night, but my tips were outstanding. I fanned my face and took a breath as I tried to get a moment to relax. But it was short-lived when Brandon decided to stand right next to me. He was too close, something I had realized he liked to do.

"A few of us are going out after work. Wanna come with?" he asked.

I shook my head and smiled. "It's been a long day. I need to get home."

"Ah, c'mon, Holland. It'll be fun."

There was something about him that grated on me and I couldn't quite place it. Was it his cockiness or his need to intrude on personal space? I didn't know why he had made it his mission to latch on to me when there were clearly others who were interested.

Milo and I had not told anyone that we were seeing each other. It was not necessarily a secret, but we hadn't discussed it either. I wanted to tell Brandon something so he would back off, but I didn't.

"Maybe another time," I finally said, pushing away from where I stood. "I need to check my tables."

I walked out of the kitchen, thankful for a reason to get distance from Brandon. And as I filled drinks, took orders, and delivered food, I kept berating myself for not being more assertive where he was concerned. He was too forward and pushy and presumptuous. But for some reason, I did not feel I could tell him to stop or back off.

Milo wasn't the reason I wanted Brandon to leave me alone, but admitting to him that there was someone else would be a way to get him to stay away.

All of my tables were doing well, so I decided to get some fresh air.

"I'm taking my break," I said to Daphne. "Is that okay?"

"Yeah. We got your tables," she said.

My phone had been buzzing all night, so I walked outside to check that everything was okay. Hendricks would have freaked out if I checked while I was on the clock, so I always had to wait. The door closed behind me as I began to scroll through the texts from my parents and Meg.

Mom: What time will you be home?

Dad: Can you bring some of that chocolate mousse home?

Meg: I had an idea for you and Milo.

I smiled at the screen, loving that Meg was as intrigued with the dating idea as I was. She was pretty creative, so I knew when she said she had an idea, it had to be a good one.

"That's a nice smile," I heard Brandon say.

I jumped as I turned to face him, shocked because I hadn't known that anyone else was outside. He was standing near the gate, about to light his cigarette when he started walking toward me. His steps were slow and deliberate, and all I could do was look at the door that led back to the kitchen.

Just go back inside.

I cleared my throat and forced my feet to move, though they felt like cinderblocks and not appendages able to carry me away. I didn't like being around Brandon; something about him always made me uncomfortable, but it was okay to overlook when others were around. At that moment, it was just Brandon and me. Alone.

It was not that I thought he would hurt me, but then again, I didn't know him well at all. We had spoken briefly over short time I had worked at the restaurant, and I was always relieved to find we were on opposite shifts. But Saturdays were an all-hands situation, so we always worked that one together.

"I should get back inside," I said as I took a step toward the door.

Brandon stopped moving and called out to me. "You okay?"

As I glanced over my shoulder to acknowledge him, I was aware of the distance from the door to where I stood. It was far. And I didn't like it.

"Yeah. I'm good," I said, trying to quell the concern in my tone. "Long day."

I started to move again when I heard his steps coming toward me.

Keep walking.

"Did I do something wrong?" he asked, and with that simple question, guilt flooded me.

"No. Of course not," I said, while the words inside my head were arguing with my mouth.

"Then why are you acting weird?" he asked as he walked the rest of the distance, brining him just a couple of feet away. "I helped with your tables, and I've tried to get you to talk to me, but you seem to be afraid of me or something."

I wanted to be snippy and tell him that he didn't know me, that he was invading my space, that he made me uncomfortable, but the words wouldn't come out.

"It's not you," I lied. "I'm just tired."

Brandon's smile grew as he took one single step toward me, bringing him so close I could hear his breathing.

"That's why you need to go out with me. Just relax and have some fun," he said. "We haven't hung out at all."

"I know…"

I didn't know what I was going to say next but then he reached out and pulled me into a tight hug. I had never really been the touchy-feely person; it took me a while to open up like that…except with Milo. But for my coworker—a stranger—to breach that space, my defenses were heightened. I lifted my hands and grabbed his shirt at his waist and tried to push him backward. When he didn't seem to notice, panic started to rise inside me and I quickly moved my hands between us and pushed against his chest.

"What's wrong?" he asked, looking hurt by my gesture.

I stared at him and briefly wondered why he would ask that. Brandon genuinely looked confused. I took a deep breath and tried to summon all of my nerve to say what I had never allowed myself to say to anyone before.

"I'm seeing someone," I said so quietly I wasn't sure that he heard. I sounded uncertain and I hated the weakness in my tone.

Really?

It was my moment—I could have told him the truth: that I didn't like to be touched by people I didn't know, that he had come on too strong, that he made me feel uncomfortable. But I froze and said the only thing I could think of at the time. And it didn't sound believable.

As I started to walk inside I heard him scoff, but I didn't bother to turn around to ask why. I was done talking, and I would no doubt spend the rest of the night replaying my lack of courage over and over.

"See you later, Holland," he said just as I opened the door.

I took a deep breath and walked back inside, making sure to plaster a convincing smile on my face.

Daphne saw me and then checked the time on the clock before smiling her approval. When I did the same, I was stunned that the entire exchange with Brandon had lasted no more than ten minutes. But it had felt like an eternity.

I needed to breathe, I needed to relax, and so I searched for the one face that would make me truly smile. When I spotted Milo with Carlo, I felt those butterflies in the pit of my stomach—the ones I got when he held my hand or kissed me. I waited for him to look in my direction, but when he didn't, disappointment replaced my momentary good mood.

"Table three is ready for their check," said Christina, one of the other servers, as she walked past me.

"Thanks. I'll get right on it."

I went to the computer and pulled up their ticket, all the while waiting for Milo to look my way. My eyes were diverted from him when I heard the back door close as Brandon walked back inside. He looked my way and offered a smile, but I ignored him, choosing to focus on my customers' request.

For the next forty-five minutes, I was busy taking orders, filling drinks, and running all over the restaurant. When I finally had a moment to be still, I walked to Milo while he was cutting some vegetables. His head was down as he concentrated on the task at hand. He really liked working with Carlo and wanted to make a good impression.

"Hey."

I leaned my back against the counter next to Milo so I could look at him, but he just continued cutting. His movements were smooth and meticulous. He cut with the skill of a seasoned chef, and I recalled the story he had shared about cooking with his mom.

"Hey," he mumbled back.

"You okay?" I asked.

He finally looked up at me, but his eyes that had looked at me the night before, filled with admiration and fun, were dull and angry. Just as I was about to push for more information, he grabbed the food he was working with and brought it to Carlo, leaving me wondering what was wrong. When he came back to his station, he still didn't acknowledge my question, causing my concern to rise.

"Milo—is something wrong?"

"No. It's fine. I have a lot to do."

"We're still going out tonight, right?"

"I don't think so, Holland," he said dismissively before walking over to grab more food to prep.

"Okay? So tomorrow?"

He set his knife down on the cutting board in front of him, moving his hands to clench the edge of the metal countertop.

I looked at him and then at the rest of the people in the kitchen, who didn't seem to notice the noise.

"Well, that sounds good. As long as you don't already have plans with Brandon," he sneered.

"Brandon? Why would I have plans with Brandon?"

"He's mentioned a few things to me…and when I went out to see you while you took your break, I decided to give you two some time since you looked so…close…out there."

"You came outside?"

Why didn't he come out and talk to me? Why didn't he save me from being alone with Brandon?

"Yeah. I guess you fell for his lines just like everyone else here."

I placed my hand on his forearm and felt his muscles tighten beneath my grasp. He looked down at my hand before meeting my eyes, and when he did, I waited until the hurt left his eyes.

"There's only one person I think I'm falling for, and it's certainly not Brandon."

He didn't say anything and I didn't wait to see if he would. Instead, I went about finishing up with my tables before my shift ended. When it was time to clock out for the day, I grabbed my things and told Daphne I was leaving. I didn't bother speaking to anyone else because I no longer felt the need to swim or hang by the club pool. I just wanted to get home. I was angry enough with myself for not making my discomfort known to Brandon, but I was also angry with Milo for assuming the worst about me.

CHAPTER 11

MILO

Walking into the house, I tossed my keys on the kitchen table and they landed with a loud thud. I kept replaying the scene in my head over and over, followed by Holland's statement about us. As soon as I looked into her eyes, I had known she was telling me the truth and I was a jerk because I had assumed the worst. We had only been out on one date and I was ruining any chances we had of a second because I was jealous.

I didn't blame her for leaving the restaurant without saying goodbye.

When I had opened the door to check on her and found Brandon with his arms around her, and I wanted to throttle the jerk. I had seen him with the other women who worked at the restaurant, and how he would lie and do whatever it took to get them to let their guard down. Holland was just another conquest to him, but to me, she was an escape from everything that confined me.

The moment I opened the door and saw his arms around her, I should have interrupted. But I knew I would have had a hard time reining in my temper. I was not a physically confrontational person, but I would have been an ass. That much I knew. And from where I stood, she looked like she was holding him. More than anything, I was pissed because she had made such a point to say we were going to give the thing between us a try. Literally the very next day, she was letting another guy hold her the way I wanted.

"What's your problem?" Dad asked as I walked into the living room.

"Nothing," I mumbled as I sat down.

He was watching the news and I stared at the screen, though I wasn't paying attention. Dad and I were a lot alike when it came to talking about feelings and things like that. He had a way of pushing for information when the time was right—something I appreciated.

"If you say so," he muttered back.

We continued watching TV, the sound from the program the only sound for a few minutes. I started to relax on the couch and tried to let go of my frustration about Brandon.

"How was work?" Dad asked.

That's how most of our conversations started. He pretended that he was distracted with something else, and then would work up the nerve to broach some topic that he thought—he knew—I needed to work out.

"Fine."

"Fine," he repeated. "You don't sound fine. Did something happen?"

"It's Holland," I finally admitted.

"What about her?" Dad asked, and then laughed lightly. "She figure out she's too good for you?"

"Probably," I scoffed.

Dad sat up straight and muted the TV as he turned to face me. I could feel his eyes burning into me as he waited for me to say more.

"I was joking, son. I thought you two were supposed to go somewhere tonight."

"Things change."

"What happened?"

"I'm just gonna go to my room and relax. It's been a long day and I'm tired," I said as I started to stand up. "I'm working the breakfast shift tomorrow."

"Now hold on, sit back down and talk to me."

"There's nothing to say, Dad. I made an ass of myself tonight."

"How so?"

I explained about seeing Brandon and Holland together and my reaction. He remained quiet while I told him about the way I had snapped at her and what she had said before she walked away. When I was done, he grinned and shook his head.

"Sounds like this Holland girl really likes you. Hell, she told you herself. So just call her up and apologize."

"Yeah, you're probably right. Maybe I will."

"Am I ever gonna get to meet this girl?" Dad asked.

"Maybe—we'll see how she feels about going out with me again."

"Grand gestures," he said.

"What?"

"Grand gestures. When you make an ass of yourself, grand gestures go a long way to make up for it. Always worked with your mom."

Dad did not mention her often, even though traces of her touches were still all over the house. Mom might have been gone, but she was still very much a fixture in our home. And when Dad needed to make a point to get me to listen, all he had to do was invoke the Mom card and there was little I could do to fight him.

"I was kind of a dick," I admitted.

"All the more reason to step up." He smirked and then turned his attention back to the news while I mulled over his advice.

I stood up abruptly and walked into the kitchen to grab my keys.

"I'll be back in a little," I said to Dad as I walked out the door.

"Good luck," he called out.

***

When I pulled up in front of her house, I started second-guessing my decision to show up uninvited. She was pretty pissed by what I had said to her at work, and why shouldn't she be? I assumed the worst. As I glanced over at the bag that was sitting on the seat next to me, I wondered if maybe it was too over the top.

"Grand gestures," I muttered out loud.

I looked at the time and hoped that her parents would not be mad that I had shown up uninvited and after ten o'clock at night. When I stepped out of the car, I walked up the sidewalk with the contents of the bag in hand but stopped midway when I saw the front door open. Holland closed the door and stood beneath the porchlight with her arms crossed.

"What are you doing here?" she asked. "It's late."

I didn't open my mouth; instead I pulled out the first card and held it up so she could read it.

Someone suggested that I apologize.

Holland took a step forward so she could read the note. When she did, she began to smile, but quickly pushed it away as I pulled out the next card.

With a grand gesture.

Her brows pinched together in confusion until I pulled out the next note that I had written out in bold black marker.

So I stole from Love Actually

(Because it was my mom's favorite movie)

96

When she read the card, the corners of her lips began to lift slightly. She seemed to relax a bit more, even dropping her arms to her side.

I'm a jerk.

"Milo," she said, but I shook my head and tossed that card to the side, revealing the next one.

I don't want to screw this up.

Holland looked at me, traces of her frustration still evident, but I could tell she was beginning of soften. Encouraged by that, I pulled out the next card.

I'm sorry.

There was something about her that made me want to make an effort. It was the only explanation for why I would show up and do something that most could possibly consider creepy. But Holland was smiling and nodded as I revealed the last card.

Please forgive me.

"Okay," she said once she read it.

"Okay? That's it?"

She shrugged her shoulders and walked toward me. On the ground at my feet was the evidence of my apology for being a jackass. She looked at the one I was still holding in my hands and took it away, tossing it to the sidewalk with the others.

"I don't like Brandon," she said.

"I know," I said, though I really had no idea how she felt about him.

"Apparently not," she said.

I reached for her hand and she allowed me to hold it. I waited for her to look me in the eyes, and when she did I moved a curl from her face that had freed itself from her ponytail.

"I've already dated the jealous guy, the jerk, the user, and the cocky guy…I just want you."

"I'm really sorry I was a jerk."

"I know." She smiled. "I read the card."

There was no reason for me to doubt anything she had said. I knew the guys she had dated while we were in school, and she had labeled each of them pretty accurately. Brandon actually fit all of those characteristics.

"Just so you know, Brandon…"

"You don't owe me any explanation," I said, knowing as I said the words, I truly believed them.

"I know. But what you saw—what you think you saw—was really him cornering me."

When her words finally registered in my mind, I felt a completely different emotion. No longer was I jealous of how Brandon held on to her; I felt a protectiveness for her. I could hear the blood rushing in my ears as I let the scenario play out in my head. Sensing my anger, Holland gently squeezed my hand, bringing me back to the present.

"He didn't hurt me."

"But you were scared."

I thought back to what I had seen when I stepped outside. She had her hands on his sides and his arms had fully enveloped her in an embrace. I had walked back inside as soon as I saw it, but maybe those hands at his side were really her trying to get some space?

When she walked into the kitchen after being alone with him, she had looked flustered. I had turned away quickly before she could see that I knew anything. Had I actually manned up, I probably would have seen that he was upset, or at the very least, concerned about what had happened with Brandon. I had seen how the women we worked with fell for him. But I had also witnessed how he treated them once the chase was over.

"I was uncomfortable," she admitted.

"I should have walked out there. I know how he is," I told her.

"I wish you would have."

"The thing is, I'm not normally a jealous person," I said.

She nodded, and something inside me pushed me to tell her the truth.

"He said some things to me the other day, and I thought that he must have gotten to you."

"Things?"

"It's nothing," I said dismissively.

"Milo."

I sighed and let go of her hand as I started to pick up the cards that I had thrown on the ground. She bent down and grabbed one of them, handing it to me when I stood up. Her eyes were wide and knew that she wasn't going to let it go.

"He knows that we know each other, but doesn't know about this," I said, motioning between the two of us.

She took my hand in hers and smiled. "Not that it's any of his business," she added.

She didn't know, but there was a part of me that wanted everyone to know about us. For years I had had feelings for Holland that I was not able to express well—or at all, considering she had thought I hated her. But now that it was happening, and we were seeing each other, I did not want us to be a secret.

"Yeah, well, he...asked me to hook the two of you up."

"Are you serious?"

I nodded, and she sighed loudly as she started walking up to the front porch, still holding my hand. When we sat down on the steps, she linked her arm with mine, threading our fingers once more.

"He asked me out tonight, and I told him I'm seeing someone."

"Did you tell him about us?"

She shook her head and looked up at me. "I didn't know if you wanted people at work to know."

I turned to fully face her, and without hesitation I cupped her face in my hand and pressed my lips against hers. She didn't hesitate returning the kiss as she held on to my arm. When I deepened the kiss, she responded by holding me tighter until we finally parted. Holland looked up into my eyes and smiled.

"I don't care who knows about us," I said through a ragged breath. "I only have a few months with you, and I don't want them to be spent in secret."

"Me either," she whispered.

I placed a chaste kiss to her lips and pulled away.

"I'm sorry we didn't get to go out tonight," I told her.

"This was better than a date," she said. "You actually opened up to me a little. I'll take that over a date anytime."

"At least the night ended the way it should."

"What, with an apology?" she teased.

I stood up and picked up the cards before helping her to her feet. She stood on a step that made her at my eye level and I wrapped my arms around her waist, kissing her one more time.

"No. With that," I said about the kiss.

She waited outside on the porch until I got into my car, and waved before I drove away. I made up my mind then and there not to miss an opportunity to be the guy that Holland deserved. And that meant I needed to open up and be honest with her.

CHAPTER 12

MILO

"Where are we going?" I asked, reaching for the blindfold over my eyes.

"Stop," he said with a laugh, pulling my hands from my eyes. "Don't peek."

"Milo," I groaned as I dropped my hands to my lap.

I could hear his amused laughter and it only made me smile despite my growing annoyance. I had loved his apology the night before and that he had been completely sincere. Milo made me feel like I was worth fighting for, and that was not something I had experienced before with anyone else. I didn't know when or how people at work would find out about us, and I did not care. When he left, a part of me hoped he would come back so we could spend more time together.

This date, whatever it was, I had been looking forward to all day. Meg and I even texted to speculate where he might be taking me. Truthfully, we could have stayed at my house and done nothing at all, and I would have been happy.

"Just a few more minutes."

As soon as we got into his car, he had handed me a blindfold, which I was not eager to put over my eyes. It was already dark outside when he picked me up, so a bathing suit seemed unnecessary. We had only been driving for about twenty minutes or so, and I knew we were still in town. I was not a fan of surprises—something I didn't realize until he blindfolded me.

"Hold on," he said as I felt the car begin to slow.

"Now?" I asked, reaching for the blindfold.

"Now."

I pulled the cover from my eyes and allowed them a moment to adjust. When they did, I could see the moon reflecting on the water. It was beautiful and peaceful, not a soul in sight. I had driven past Stephens Lake many times, but I never stopped to enjoy it. I was always more of a beach kind of girl.

"Have you ever gone swimming at night?" he asked.

Slowly I shook my head and looked over at him. All my fears, real and completely irrational, were beginning to choke me.

"No." It was the only thing I was able to eke out.

"You don't like it," he questioned, but it was more of an observation.

"I'm terrified," I admitted.

"But you can swim, right?"

I laughed, thankful he had lightened the mood. I nodded and turned my attention toward the dark abyss in front of me.

"What scares you?"

"Whatever might be in the water. Like the Loch Ness Monster."

Milo laughed and reached for my hand. "Not real."

"I know that," I scoffed. "Doesn't make me any less scared."

"I'll protect you."

Milo opened his door, and reluctantly I opened my own. As I stepped out of the car I felt the fear travel up my spine, but I wanted to overcome it. He stood at the front of his car and waited for me to join him. Every step I took toward Milo felt heavier than the last until I finally reached him. He took my hand in his and carried a large backpack over his other shoulder.

"What's the bag for? Are you going to kill me?"

Milo threw his head back and laughed hard. "You're awesome. And no. It's towels and some snacks."

"Why night swimming? Isn't it dangerous?"

"Well yeah…that's why it's the perfect date," he answered.

My stomach flipped, and not because he was holding my hand. I found my nerves were working overtime and a flood of possibilities came to mind.

"Doesn't sound so perfect."

"Trust me," he said as we continued to walk.

When we got to the shore, the water looked like glass, barely a breeze to make the surface move. Milo spread out a large blanket and set the backpack on top of it while I looked out at the horizon. In the distance, I could see the lights shining from homes across the way. The lake had few public spots that were accessible, and the park always closed at ten. I glanced at my watch and sighed because it was only eight. We had plenty of time to drown before anyone found us.

Milo pulled off his T-shirt and tossed it to the side by the bag. I tried not to look, but when I was caught staring at his stomach, I was thankful for the moonlit darkness.

"Are you going to get in?" he asked.

"I'm not sure."

I figured he would be frustrated or that he would sulk because I didn't jump at the chance to go with him. Instead, he walked over and kissed my cheek before walking toward the water.

As he took his first steps into the inky darkness, I watched his figure, admiring the way the moon illuminated his physique. Milo was not one to show off the muscles that he wore beneath his clothing, but they were on full display for me. I wanted so badly to follow him and let go of my fears, but all I could think of were the wild creatures that I saw in movies.

"It's a little chilly," he said as he stood waist deep, looking back at me.

"Not helping," I laughed.

"Not trying to," he answered with a chuckle.

I grabbed one of the towels that he had set out and opened it up so I could sit down. The warm air covered my body and I started to sweat. Maybe I was sweating because I was nervous, but whatever the reason I began to grow increasingly warm. Milo was still walking deeper into the water when I took off my cover-up, revealing my black bikini.

"Grow up," I muttered to myself, hoping to gain some courage.

"How you doin' over there?" Milo asked from the water.

"Great," I said unconvincingly before laughing softly. "How 'bout you?"

"Not too bad."

His body disappeared beneath the water and I watched, waiting for him to come to the surface. When he didn't come up right away, I sat up a little taller to see if there were any ripples in the water. Panic began to course through my veins and I started to get up as I searched for him in the darkness.

"Milo?" I called out, trying to contain my fear.

I walked toward the shoreline, the water lapping at my feet. Just as I started to take a step in, he surfaced with a loud splash.

"That was crazy," he called out.

"You scared me! I was just about to get in to find you."

Milo stilled in the water and faced where I stood with my arms crossed over my chest.

"You look amazing," he said breathlessly. "Wow."

I dropped my hands to cover my stomach, even though there wasn't enough light for him to see much of my body. I had always been a little self-conscious of the small scar I had from my appendectomy. It was the first time I had bought a swimsuit that had the potential of showing the mark on my stomach because of how low the bottoms were. But Meg had convinced me to buy it when we were trying on clothes before school got out.

I started to back away from the edge and Milo stayed quiet. He was not going to try to pressure me to do something that scared me, and I appreciated that. When I stopped moving, we stared at each other and I began to slowly move my hands to my sides, no longer hiding the scar. I took a deep breath and pushed myself forward toward the water.

"Do you want me to come get you?" he asked.

"I'm okay," I answered, taking the timid steps toward him.

The water was cool against my skin, and with every inch that I sank, goose bumps traveled the length of my body. Every time a creature—real or made up—came to mind, I tried to take a deep breath and be brave. It was hard to do, because my imagination was working overtime. Milo remained in place, watching out for me as I continued my trek into the water.

Finally, I bent my knees and let the water fall over my shoulders as I swam toward where he stood. When I got close enough, he reached out his hand for me and pulled me toward him, holding me near his side. The shoes protected my feet from the rocks on the lake floor, but I started to freak out and grabbed ahold of his shoulders as I lifted my feet.

"Things in the water," I mumbled my excuse.

"I got ya," he said as he placed his hands on the sides of my stomach.

"Yeah. I think you do."

My hands snaked around his neck as he started to pull me closer. I was about to have, probably, the most romantic kiss I had ever had when something slapped against my leg.

"What was that?" I yelled.

In one swift maneuver, I moved to his back, holding on to his neck as tightly as I could. Milo tapped at my arm to loosen my grip, but I was terrified as I wrapped my legs around his waist.

"Something touched my leg," I said desperately.

"It was probably just a fish," he said calmly. "It's fine."

"Says you," I said, still holding tightly to him.

It was then that I realized I was skin to skin, alone in the darkness with this guy and it was only our second date. I started to loosen my grip from his neck, my hands resting on his shoulders. The moon was behind us and he couldn't see my face, which I was certain had turned a scary shade of red from the thoughts in my mind.

"Holland?" he asked quietly.

"Yeah?"

His hand covered mine as he helped me swim so I could face him. When we were face to face once more, his features were revealed by the reflection of the moon on the water. He was beautiful.

"Something just touched my leg," he said with a startle that made me jump.

I started to swim back to shore, but he grabbed my hand and pulled me back to him with a laugh. I was momentarily confused, until I realized that he was playing a joke on me.

"I'm sorry, I couldn't help it," he said through his laughter.

"You're a terrible person," I scolded as splashed water at him, but it only made him laugh harder. "I can't believe you're laughing. You knew I was scared."

Milo was still laughing until I decided to get even by dunking him under water. I pushed myself up and shoved him beneath the surface, swimming toward the shore as I laughed. I felt his hand wrap around my ankle as he attempted to stop my retreat. Before I knew it, he was once again in front of me, his face dripping wet.

"I'm so going to get you back for this," I told him as I started to laugh while I held on to his shoulders.

He reached out his hand and moved a piece of hair from my face, his smile beginning to fade. I watched how his eyes moved from where his hand touched my face and then to my lips. My legs were wrapped around his waist as his hands held on to me. I was, once again, aware of the skin-to-skin contact, the heat of his shoulders radiating to my hands.

The moment his lips touched mine, I was no longer afraid of what might be in the water. I was more concerned with how his lips and his hands made me forget everything else around me. My hands slid around his neck as his mouth explored mine. And as our kiss began to slow, I became more aware of how much he affected me—not just in the way his touch felt, but in the way he looked at me and spoke.

"This scares me," I admitted when we parted.

"Me too," he said.

I untangled myself from his body and stood on the lake floor as I tried to rein in all I was feeling. We walked to the shore, hand in hand, and toweled off in silence. I was at a loss for words, though a part of me wanted to tell him everything I was feeling at that moment. Instead, I sat down I stared up at the countless stars overhead as he rifled through his bag.

"It's beautiful out here," I said as I lay down to get a better view of the night sky.

"I'm glad you like it, too."

I patted the free spot next to me, and Milo stopped whatever it was he had been doing and joined me. Instead of looking up at the stars, he propped himself up on his left arm and stared down at me.

"Why are you looking at me like that?" I asked.

"How am I looking at you?"

"I'm not sure," I chuckled. "But you're making me nervous."

Milo started to move away, but I reached for his free hand to stop him. He lowered his face to mine and kissed me briefly. His free hand traced lazy circles on my forearm as we looked at the stars. I was keenly aware of his body's proximity to mine and how his fingers warmed every inch of flesh they touched. But I froze the moment he grazed the scar on my stomach.

"What's that from?" he asked quietly.

"Appendectomy when I was ten," I answered as I fought the urge to cover it. "I don't ever wear bikinis because of it."

"Why?"

"Why?" I scoffed. "Because I'm an eighteen-year-old girl who has a scar on her stomach."

"So? We all have scars. No one is perfect."

"Yeah but…"

"No buts. It's just something else that makes you special. And I happen to think you're beautiful—and this," he said, gently brushing his finger against the raised, scarred flesh, "is too."

I looked into his eyes, trying to find evidence that he was handing me a line, but I couldn't see it. As I pushed myself to sit up, Milo moved back slightly to give me space until I was upright. He started to move away, but I grabbed his arm to stop him. I wanted to thank him for what he had said. I wanted to say *something*, but words failed me, so I kissed him.

When we parted, the silence began to stretch between us and began to weigh heavy on me. With every second that passed, a sense of dread overcame me and I almost wished I was back in the waters that terrified me. At least in the water, I sort of knew what I was getting into, but with Milo it was all uncharted territory.

He reached into his bag and handed a bottle of water to me before taking one for himself.

The air was heavy with unspoken words, and if I had known the perfect thing to say to break it, I would have said it. Instead, I sat there next to him and hoped that maybe we didn't have to speak. Maybe we could just start making out again.

"Just so you know, I'm not expecting anything," Milo said, breaking the quiet.

I took another sip of my drink and nodded before meeting his eyes.

"I wish I could say the same," I admitted. "But something tells me this is going to end with a broken heart."

Milo closed his eyes and sighed, setting his drink down. As he shifted his position on the blanket, I noticed that he seemed to be a bit fidgety. He grabbed the back of his neck and finally made eye contact with me again. Whatever was going on in his head was bothering him, but I allowed him time to say whatever it was he needed to say.

"There's something I should tell you," he said, and I set my drink down. He took a deep breath and looked at me. "When you leave at the end of the summer, I'll still be here."

"What do you mean?"

"College. I'm not going. At least not right now," he said.

"You were in the top of our class," I reminded him, as if he didn't already know his rank.

"Yeah."

"Okay...but I thought you said..."

"I know what I let you think," he interrupted. "But I didn't want you to think I was a loser."

"A loser? Why would I think that? College isn't for everyone," I said.

"That's just it. I want to go, but it's not feasible."

"I'm sorry, Milo," I said, reaching for his hand, but he pulled it away.

"No. That's what I mean. I don't want you to feel sorry for me, okay? It is what it is. I have a few things that I'm working out, and I'll be taking some classes at the junior college in the meantime. I just didn't want to have this secret out there, looming over my head. I needed to be honest with you."

"You know there are other ways."

He shook his head and grinned. "I appreciate what you're saying, but..."

"If you want to go..."

"Seriously, you need to drop it. Would it be the worst thing if I wasn't able to go to college? Would you think less of me or something?"

His question stunned me, because that was not at all what I meant to imply. Of course, in my overzealous attempt to advise, it sounded otherwise, and I needed for him to hear me. I shook my head slowly and looked him in the eyes, and tried with all my heart to communicate what I was thinking.

"Milo Davis, I think you're ridiculously smart and talented. I've always been impressed by you, before I even really knew you. And I have no doubt you're going to be amazing at whatever it is you decide to do. Now, that aside, can I be honest with you?" I asked, and he nodded for me to continue. "I'm going to spend this summer with you and I'm probably going to fall in love with you. And my heart is going to be crushed when it's over."

He chuckled softly and shook his head. "Then why do it?"

I pushed myself closer to where he sat so my face was inches away. "Because, I don't think it's *feasible* for me to stay away from you," I said before kissing him again.

CHAPTER 13

MILO

Holland and I had spent nearly every day of the past two weeks together. I felt a sense of relief since I had shared with her that I was not going to college. I didn't go into detail, but she seemed to understand anyway. We had been working opposite shifts for the last week, but had managed to see each other in between. Seeing Holland became the best part of my day.

It was a Tuesday evening before we were scheduled to work together, and I suggested that I pick her up so we could go out after our shifts ended. It was the first time that people at work would really know that we were a couple. It was not a secret, but it seemed weird to make some big announcement about it. Though admittedly, the idea of Brandon finally being shut down was a huge bonus.

"What's the plan after work?" I asked.

"I'm up for anything," Holland answered as we pulled into the parking lot at Pine Bridge.

"Even coming to my house?" I asked.

I turned the engine off and got out of the car. Holland stepped out from the passenger seat and grabbed her things before closing the door and meeting me near the trunk. Sometimes I would look at her and her smile would catch me off guard. I was still amazed that somehow we had ended up together after I had spent so much time thinking it would never happen.

"Do I get to meet your dad?" she asked.

I reached down for her hand and lifted it to my lips, kissing the top of her hand. "He's off today."

"Really?" she asked, smiling excitedly. "I can't wait to meet him."

"Fair warning, he's not exactly Mr. Friendly."

"Shocked," she scoffed. "Neither are you."

She started to laugh and let go of my hand as she jogged slightly ahead of me. I hurried after her and wrapped my arm around her waist when I was close enough. Her hands were on my shoulders and she was still smiling as I hugged her against me.

Holland always smelled like summer—that combination of sea air and suntan oil. I kissed her once and released my hold of her just as the back door to the kitchen swung open, revealing a moody Brandon. He must have seen me first because his narrowed glare and scowl were fixed solely on me until he caught sight of Holland. Immediately he softened and smiled when he saw that she was smiling.

"Hey, Holl," he said, and her smile faded.

"Holland," she corrected.

Brandon seemed to ignore her and turned his attention to me. "I think Chef was looking for you."

He was full of it. Carlo and I had already discussed the menu for the day, and he certainly would not send Brandon out to find me. Though I thought it was mostly coincidence that he had ended up outside where Holland and I were.

"Yeah, I'll check in with him in a minute," I said dismissively, and then turned to Holland. "I'm very friendly."

She threw her head back and laughed, slapping at my arm.

Brandon took the two steps from the door to stand where we were and crossed his arms, looking between the two of us.

"What's going on?" he asked Holland, trying to block me from the conversation.

"Inside joke," she said with a shrug.

"Aw c'mon. Tell me," he prodded.

Holland looked at me and smirked like she knew exactly what

she was doing. She shrugged her shoulders and nodded her chin in my direction. "I was just telling Milo he must get his personality from his dad."

"That's not what you said," I laughed, stepping closer to her.

Brandon was looking between the two of us as we chuckled and argued about who was right. His smile began to fade when he realized that he was not making any headway with Holland. She had moved closer to me while we bantered, moving herself away from him. And in case he had not already gotten the hint, Holland stood right in front of me and pointed her finger against my chest before kissing me briefly.

"I win," she said proudly when she managed to shut me up with her mouth.

She moved away, still looking directly into my eyes, and she raised a brow. Holland knew exactly what she was doing, and I could not have been happier. She bit her bottom lip before turning around where we were face to face with a stunned Brandon. I threaded my fingers with hers and she squeezed gently as Brandon's shock turned to disgust.

"Are you two together?" he sneered.

"Yeah," she answered snappishly. "Why?"

Brandon shook his head and turned around before walking back inside without another word. The metal door slammed hard behind him and Holland flinched at the sound. I was still holding her hand and tugged her to me, kissing the tip of her nose when she was standing in front of me once more. I never tired of looking into those brown eyes.

"That was fun," she whispered.

I leaned in to kiss her cheek and whispered, "You told him we're together."

"Well, we are. No sense in making people think otherwise." She shrugged.

She grabbed a hair tie from her wrist and pulled her hair up out of her face. Her usual white button-down shirt was replaced with the sleeveless polo that the waitstaff wore when they were working the poolside grill. It was a clear blue June day and it was the first time Holland was getting to work outdoors. She had been hoping to get out of the formal dining area since she started, and when her name was listed, she had been thrilled.

"Let's get inside so we can clock in," I said.

As I held the door open for her, several heads turned, their eyes fixed on us. Brandon was near the entrance to the main dining area and stood with his arms crossed over his chest. He was not a happy guy when he did not get his way, and Holland was one name he would not be adding to his list of conquests.

Daphne walked over and looked at the two of us, but fixed her attention on Holland. I respected her because she was fair and made it a point to treat everyone well. She had put up with hell from both Hendricks and Carlo, but her even temper made her an asset to the restaurant.

"You two are dating?" she asked, almost in monotone.

"Yes," Holland answered in the same manner.

"Okay," Daphne responded before turning around and calling the staff together about a new menu item.

Holland stood next to me and listened while Daphne spoke for a few minutes. When she was done, she dismissed everyone to their respective stations and did not say another word about Holland and me.

"That was easy," Holland said when we had a moment to ourselves. "I guess I better get outside."

"Have fun," I answered.

She leaned in to kiss me and realized we were at work, so she left me with a smile instead. When she had disappeared to the outdoor kitchen area, Jaysen walked over and patted my shoulder.

"Good for you."

"Thanks?" I said, though it sounded more like a question.

"I was wondering what was going on with you. You've been unusually…happy."

"Happy?"

"You've at least been in a better mood," he said with a laugh. "Happy for you, man."

"Thanks."

Carlo walked over to Jaysen and me and began talking to us about what the plan was for the special. It was a salmon dish he'd talked about recreating numerous times, but he wasn't sure that the guests would be up for it. Ultimately he had decided that if he tried it on one of the slower days and people didn't respond to it as he hoped, then he would not serve it again.

"Milo, I need you to go into the back and grab some extra pans for the fish," Carlo said.

"Got it," I answered as I hurried to the back.

As I rounded the corner, I heard Brandon talking to someone in Hendricks' office, his voice tinged with anger. It wasn't uncommon to find him complaining about something. Usually it was about his shift, or having to memorize the specials, so I thought nothing of it until I heard him mention Holland's name.

"That's bullshit," he spat. "You lectured me for dating Monique, but this is allowed?"

I was shocked that he would speak to Hendricks so harshly, because she would not hesitate to fire him on the spot. I may have not been the boss's biggest fan, but she had never done anything to offend me and I tended to stay out of her way.

"Listen Brandon…"

When I heard her voice, I knew he was complaining to Daphne. She was the only other female there who had not fallen for Brandon's act. And that was just another reason to respect her.

"You know I'm right, Daph. If you're going to make the rules, you need to enforce them."

"You need to calm down. You don't get to tell me how to run my kitchen. If you have a problem with it, take it up with Hendricks."

"Fine," he grumbled.

I set about getting the supplies that Carlo had requested, thankful that Daphne had my back. There were other couples who worked at the restaurant; not everyone was so open about it. The only reason anyone knew about Holland and me was because of Brandon. The rule he mentioned was in place *because* of him. He had caused so much drama by dating and dumping the women we worked with when he had gotten what he wanted from them.

With all the items in hand, I walked back to Carlo, but not before I heard the Daphne's parting words to Brandon.

"What are mad about?" she asked. "That she's with Milo or that she rejected you?"

"She didn't reject me," he argued. "And that's not the point."

"That's fine. You need to get back to work," she said, dismissing him.

He stormed out of the office and pushed past me with more

force than was necessary. Brandon was used to getting his way and I had had enough of his attitude.

"Watch it," I called after him, and he stopped dead in his tracks.

I wasn't some scrawny guy he could push around, but because I was usually quiet, he thought he thought I was easy to railroad. My temper rarely got the best of me, but when it did, it was for a pretty good reason. At that moment he had been badmouthing Holland—someone who had done nothing but politely reject him.

"Someone grew some balls," he sneered as he turned to face me.

"You need to walk away," I warned.

"Or what?"

I shook my head slowly and walked toward Carlo with the things he needed to get started. As I walked past Brandon I heard him mumble something under his breath, but I was not sure what he said.

"Care to repeat that?" I asked.

Brandon faced me and crossed his arm over his chest, trying to intimidate me. There was nothing about him that concerned me, other than I wanted to knock the hell out of him to get him to shut up. But I was not alone in that thought. Jaysen hated the guy.

"I bet you wouldn't be so cocky if you knew what she was really like. But you go ahead and pretend that she's not sloppy seconds."

After calmly setting the pans on the counter behind me, I shoved him against the wall and watched as the color drained from his face. Brandon had never seen that side of me before; not many had, and there was never a better time to show it.

"If you *ever* talk about her like that again, disrespect her, or even so much as look at her, I will knock your ass out. Got it?" I said through clenched teeth.

Brandon maintained his calm, but from the way he avoided looking me in the eyes, I knew he was nervous. Slowly he nodded his head, and I released my hold of him before picking up the pans and walking back to Carlo as if nothing had happened. And as long as Brandon left Holland alone, everything would be fine.

"What the hell was that?" Jaysen asked as I set everything on the counter.

I looked over my shoulder where Brandon had been and shrugged. Jaysen had seen the whole thing, and I thought I had done a pretty good job of being discreet. In reality I had done what everyone else had wanted to do for a long time, and that was to put Brandon in his place.

"You need to watch it," Jaysen warned. "I know you don't like the guy, but you need to be careful."

"I think we understand each other. It's all good," I said.

"If you say so."

CHAPTER 14

HOLLAND

By the time our shifts ended, my feet were killing me and I was certain that I smelled like a sweaty little boy in need of a shower. Milo was supposed to take me to his house to hang out, but I really wanted a shower.

"You can use our shower," he said. "It's clean. I promise."

I laughed, and though I really wanted to go home, I agreed.

As we drove to his house, he told me about his dad and how he had been picking up extra shifts. He never said why, but it was my understanding that the two of them made a great team in making sure everything on the home front ran smoothly.

I waited for him to mention the confrontation with Brandon, but he never did. I had heard about it from Steph, one of the girls who was working the Patio Grill with me. She was a bit fuzzy with the details, but from the little she was able to share, Brandon had complained to Daphne or Hendricks about our relationship. When I asked Steph if I would get in trouble, she shook her head and assured me that Brandon was the problem, not Milo or me.

"I'm starving," I said as my stomach began to rumble.

Milo smiled and pointed down the road. "Last house on the right. I'll make you something to eat while you get cleaned up."

"You're the best."

"Anything for you," he answered.

We pulled into the driveway and he put the car in park but made no move to get out right away. I knew he was about to tell me what had happened with Brandon, so I waited patiently while he worked up to it.

At least that was what I was expecting. His hands gripped the wheel and he stared at the house, the car completely silent. I reached for his hand, and he turned his head to look at me, a hint of a smile present. I loved the way he looked at me; it made my heart pound rapidly every time. I never wanted that feeling to go away. He opened his mouth like he was about to say something, but instead I caught his eyes darting to my lips before meeting my eyes again. He closed the space between us, his hand holding the back of my neck, his full lips brushing softly against mine. It was so perfect.

When we parted, he opened his door to get out of the car and I knew then that he had no plans to mention the incident with Brandon. If I wanted to know about it, I was going to have to ask, and a part of me was perfectly fine not knowing.

I expected to walk into a house that screamed *two men live here*, but that was not what I saw. The walls were light beige with dark gray wood floors, and there were pictures on all the walls. The feminine touches were evident, and I knew those were the traces of his mom that he had mentioned to me before. The light brown furniture was adorned with light blue and green pillows that matched the curtains over the windows.

"Your house is so nice," I gushed.

"What did you expect?" he teased.

"Guys? I don't know," I laughed. "Where's your dad?"

"He should be home in about an hour. You want something to drink?"

We walked into the kitchen and I noticed a picture of an older man and woman smiling as they held a younger boy who I immediately recognized as Milo.

"You look a lot like your mom," I said, pointing to the picture.

"Yeah, that's what everyone always told her. She loved hearing that," he said with a smile. "I may look like her, but I'm probably more like my dad than I'd like to admit."

"How so?"

"We tend to stay quiet, wanting to do things our way. And neither of us are big on other people's opinions."

"Has he dated anyone since your mom died?" I asked, unsure if it was an appropriate question to ask.

Milo shook his head and grabbed two waters from the refrigerator, handing one to me. We sat down at the round kitchen table and he remained quiet before gulping his water.

"Maybe now that I've listened to him, he'll return the favor," Milo joked.

"Listened to him?"

He scoffed and leaned back in his chair with a smirk on his face. "Dad was the one who told me to tell you about college. He wasn't exactly thrilled when he found out."

"Wait, what? He didn't know you weren't going to college?"

"He didn't know that I even applied."

Applied?

That little bit of information had been omitted from our conversation. When he had mentioned that it was not feasible for him to go to college, I had thought it was a money situation, or maybe he didn't get in, but I chose not to ask because it was not my business.

"Where did you apply?"

"A few locals like Westview, Stonewall, and Mount Pleasant. Then a few out of state."

"And?" I asked, waiting for more information.

"And what?"

"Did you hear back?"

"Yeah. Got into all of them."

My head was swimming with his revelation. Milo had not only applied to college, but had gotten into all of them? I knew he was smart—top ten percent gets you into most of the schools in Texas—but even out of state? I was simultaneously impressed and confused. When I finally looked at him, he watched me with hurt or disappointment in his eyes. It was hard to tell what he was feeling because I found it hard to get a read on him.

"Don't look at me like that, please," he said.

"How am I looking at you?"

"Don't feel sorry for me. That's the last thing I want."

"If you got into all of the schools you applied to, why are you going to the junior college?"

As soon as I asked the question, I knew the answer. I regretted the tone in my asking, but it was out there, heavy in the space between us.

"I'll get there," he said, reaching across the table for my hand. "I'm saving up and I'm going to make it happen. But let's not talk about this in front of my dad, okay?"

"Okay."

He released a breath and smiled as he sat back, satisfied that the conversation was over, at least for the moment.

"Did I tell you that this is the first time I've ever brought anyone home to my dad?"

"Really? Why is that?"

"Honestly?" he asked, and I nodded. "Well, don't freak out or anything, but really, I've just never liked anyone enough to bring them home."

"You know what I wish? I wish I could redo senior year," I said.

"Why the hell would you want to do that?"

"Not the tests or any of the other crap, but you. I wish I could go back and make you talk to me, get to know you then like I know you now. Have those conversations with you that I was always too nervous to have," I said.

121

"Like?"

"Like...what are you doing this weekend? Or...did you see the game last night?"

"Do you have a date to prom?" he asked.

"Exactly."

"But at least we have the summer together."

"True," I said, forcing a smile, though it made me sad to think that any of it would end.

"And we have our bucket list, right?"

Milo stood up and walked toward me, helping me to my feet. He wrapped his arms around my waist and looked down at me with so much sweetness.

"If I tell you that I like you, is that going to freak you out?" he asked.

"I hope you like me, considering we've made out quite a bit," I laughed.

"That's true."

I pushed up on my tiptoes and kissed him briefly before settling back to my aching feet.

"I like you too," I whispered, and then felt my cheeks begin to flush and I added, "A lot more than like."

"Same, Holland."

How could I feel so much so quickly? When I was with Blake, I was never completely sure that when I told him I loved him, I meant it. I was hurt when he dumped me, but it was more ego than sad to be without him. What I was already feeling for Milo scared me. Was it possible to love someone when you had only really spent time with them for two weeks?

He was looking down at me like something was weighing on his mind, but whatever it was, he chose not to talk about it. And I decided not to press the issue. Milo would open up to me when he was ready, and I knew the same was true for me.

"C'mon, I'll show you the bathroom," he said, reaching for my hand and leading me to a hallway.

He grabbed a towel from a closet in the hallway and handed it to me before guiding me to a bedroom. There, I saw a glimpse into Milo that I had only imagined. His room was immaculate, a navy blue comforter laid over a queen-sized bed. There was a plain wooden desk near the window where his computer was set between two neat stacks of papers.

"Are you a neat freak?" I teased.

"Nah. I cleaned it last night."

"For me?"

He smiled and walked to his dresser where he pulled out some clothes and handed them to me.

"It's a T-shirt and shorts. The shorts will be too big, but there's a drawstring," he said.

"You're so sweet," I said. "Thank you."

I took all the items he had handed me and disappeared into the bathroom to clean up so I would look presentable when I met his dad.

***

"This is good pizza," I said to Mr. Davis.

He had arrived home shortly after I got out of the shower. It probably looked a little suspicious that I was wearing Milo's things and my wet hair was a mess. Clearly I did not truly consider what constituted "presentable."

"So Milo tells me you're going to Westview. That's a good school."

"Yes, sir. I'm going to study business."

"Good for you. How do you like working out there at the country club?"

"It's not too bad. Most of the people there are pretty great. And working with Milo helps."

Mr. Davis smiled and looked at his son. He seemed to choose his words carefully when he spoke, something I noticed Milo did too. We continued to finish up our meal and I helped Milo clear the plates. Mr. Davis had gone to his room to get cleaned up while Milo and I went into the living room to watch a movie.

It was the first time we had sat around and did absolutely nothing, and it felt pretty nice. My parents were going away for the weekend, so I did not have to worry about waking them up when I got home.

"Hey, I'll be back," Milo said.

He got up and kissed the top of my head, and I watched as he started to walk away.

"Where are you going?"

"I need to clean up. I feel like I smell salmon on me."

I laughed. "I didn't notice, but whatever."

He smiled and walked down the hallway and disappeared around the corner. The movie had not really kept my attention, but I would glance at the screen from time to time when I was not looking at the family pictures on the wall. Milo had the same dark hair and eyes as his mom, but his smile was the same as his dad.

"Beautiful, isn't she?" Mr. Davis asked when he saw me looking at one of the pictures of his wife.

"She really is," I answered.

He sat down on the worn leather recliner that was next to me and started to watch the movie with me. As he rocked the chair in a slow, smooth motion, I turned my attention back to the television.

"Milo said he told you about college."

"Yes, sir. He did."

"I'm glad. Secrets can really ruin a relationship."

"I agree."

"And I guess you two have thought about what happens at the end of the summer when you leave?"

His question sat heavy in my heart, because I had thought about it, and it hurt. Milo and I chose to ignore the elephant in the room most of the time, but it was always there. And knowing that he had gotten into Westview but decided not to accept gutted me. We could have been there together in the fall.

"I'm sorry," he said as he shook his head. "Milo asked me not to bring it up so I didn't upset you."

I sat upright and faced Mr. Davis, who looked at me. "He told *me* not to bring it up to *you*."

"That boy," he muttered as he looked toward the hall where Milo had gone to get cleaned up. "Let's go outside and get some fresh air."

I readily agreed and followed him to the back yard, where we sat on the back porch. The yard was not very big, but it had a beautiful garden on the far back end.

"My wife planted those when we moved here."

"It's so pretty."

"I just found out a couple of weeks ago that he applied anywhere. And he got in."

"It's great that he has so many options."

"Well, he would have if he had accepted any of them," Mr. Davis said. "He never talked about college. Every time I brought it up, he'd say he had homework or something else."

"He told me that it wasn't a feasible option for him," I repeated from our conversation at the lake.

Mr. Davis scrubbed his hand over his face and then crossed his arms. I could tell that what I had said resonated with him. Milo was deliberate in what he chose to share with me, and it seemed he was the same with his dad.

Milo stepped outside, looking between his dad and me.

"Got tired of the movie?" he asked.

I looked at Mr. Davis and shrugged. "It's too nice tonight not to sit out here and enjoy it."

"And you were right, Hollz," Mr. Davis said, and I smiled. There were few people who called me by my nickname, and I liked that he used it. "I'm going inside to get some water. You two want something?"

"I'm fine, thank you," I answered as he stepped back inside the house, leaving Milo and me alone again.

As Milo sat down in the chair next to mine, he leaned over and kissed my cheek. He looked down at me and smirked.

"I like seeing you in my shirt," he said.

"Easy, mister. Your dad is right there. I'm sure this whole look I'm sportin' right now makes me look completely guilty of something I didn't even do."

"Guilty, huh?"

"Yeah, speaking of…are you ever going to tell me about what happened with Brandon?"

"You heard about that?"

"You're kidding, right?"

Milo squeezed his eyes shut and shook his head. "Steph?"

"Yep."

He reached for my hand and looked apologetic. I was glad the truth about the two of us was out there, and relieved to know that Daphne would not hold it against me. I had managed to avoid Brandon for the rest of the day, and from the sound of it, that was for the best.

"I don't know what you heard, but I just had a little talk with him and told him to back off."

"Okay."

"Okay? Are you pissed?"

"Should I be?"

"No…I was just looking out for you."

I smiled at Milo and nodded. "I know. And I would do the same for you."

Little did I realize that I had already taken that step, just in talking to his dad about college. But I would worry about that later. I just hoped that he liked me enough not to hold it against me.

CHAPTER 15

HOLLAND

While I managed to enjoy the night swim in the lake, a chlorinated body of water like the one in my back yard was more my speed. Since it was my day off, I spent the whole day outside by the pool and came up with ideas of things to do with Milo. Luckily, I remembered a conversation I had had with my friend Colin the week before and I knew exactly what I wanted to do.

"Coffee and puppies? Is that really a thing?" Milo asked.

He was reading the sign beneath Café Bark as we pulled into a gravel parking lot. It was an old house that had been renovated into a coffee shop. There were several dog houses placed in the front of the house, with signs that labeled them as "barking lots." The small aqua house was decorated with bright flowers and whimsical toys that the animals seemed to enjoy.

"You like dogs, right?" I asked.

I got out of my car and tucked the keys inside my purse that was slung across my chest. Milo walked over to the front of my car and narrowed his eyes at me.

"Who doesn't like dogs?"

"Good answer." I smiled.

"You don't even like coffee," Milo said.

"I know…but I love dogs."

I was one of the few people I knew who had never acquired a taste for coffee. It was too strong and gross; even if someone tried to sweeten it, I still refused to drink it. But I would find something I liked just to be with man's best friend.

Off to the side of the house was a grassy area that was a fenced off with a small gate to access it. Six bistro tables were scattered throughout the space, and I noticed some people sitting, enjoying their drinks. Milo opened the gate for me and we took a seat at one of the empty tables.

Just as I was about to comment on the clear, blue day, a little ball of fur came running toward us and I squealed so loud that several heads turned to see what was happening.

"I'm sorry," I said as I sank to my knees and Milo laughed.

The beige and white puppy was jumping all over me and licking my face when his little friend joined in. They were quite the pair, clearly from the same litter. My heart could barely handle all the cuteness, and I looked up to see Milo taking a picture of me with the puppies.

"They're so cute," I gushed, and Milo agreed.

He finally joined me on the ground and the puppies moved to share the love with him. I could tell he liked them just as much as me, and listening to him talk to the puppies was so adorable.

"We're never leaving this place, are we?" Milo joked.

"Nope. I think"—I reached to read the name tag on the first puppy—"Lima wants us to stay."

Milo read the tag of the puppy he was holding and smiled. "Yeah, same for Bean."

"Lima and Bean?" I repeated. "That's so cute!"

"Yeah, they're a handful," an older woman said as she approached our table.

I laughed and stood up, wiping my hands on my shorts. Milo seemed perfectly content on the ground, so I sat down and took the menu the woman offered.

"I'm Sarah, and I'll be taking care of you today. Can I get you some water while you look over the menu?"

"That would be great," I said.

"This must be your first time here," she said as she looked down at Milo.

"It is," I said.

"Well, just a little about us: we are a shelter that doubles as a coffee shop."

"Shelter? I didn't realize that."

"Oh yes. We love our babies here, but they're all adoptable. And of course, many of our customers love to bring their own furbabies when they come. Okay, if you need anything just let me know, and I'll be right back with your waters."

Sarah walked away and I looked around at the puppies that were running around in the yard. Some were older and much more docile, but Lima and Bean were clearly the babies. The two took off running toward an older lab that was lying near the fence, enjoying the sun. They jumped on top of the dog and started biting on its ears until the dog rolled over onto its back and then they started climbing all over it.

"That's so sad," I said when I looked at Milo. "All these puppies need homes?"

"Sounds like it."

"I wish I could take them all."

"Did you have any pets growing up?" he asked.

"Yeah, I had a dog and a cat. Maybe and Chicken."

"Maybe chicken what?"

"No," I laughed. "Those were their names. Maybe was our pug and Chicken was our cat."

"You had a cat named Chicken?"

"Yeah, my dad thought it would be funny."

"So what happened to them? I didn't see any pets when I went to your house before."

"Maybe died a while back. And Chicken got out of the house one day and never came home."

"I'm sorry," he said sweetly.

"What about you?"

"We had a German shepherd before my mom died. We always talked about getting another dog, but never did."

I had never known loss like Milo had experienced. The closest person to me to die was my grandmother, but I was four and could barely remember it. The thought of losing my parents was enough to bring me to tears, but there I was sitting with Milo, who had lost one of the most important people in his life.

"Don't look at me like that," Milo said, forcing a smile.

"How am I looking at you?"

"It's fine. I'm okay talking about her."

"What was she like? You told me she was a terrible cook, but tell me something else."

"She was engaged to someone else before she met my dad."

"She was?"

"Yep."

He nodded his head as if he was thinking about the story, and then he looked off to where the puppies were still playing with the bigger dog. I hoped that he would tell me more, but it was almost as if he had just shut down. When he looked at me again, he was smiling.

"She left him for my dad."

"Did she ever say why?"

"She knew him from church—I think my dad was a bit of a troublemaker. And one day something just clicked and she fell for him."

"Your dad a troublemaker, huh?"

"I never met my grandfather, but from what my mom said, he wasn't a nice guy. And it almost didn't happen with Mom and Dad."

"Why?"

He shrugged. "She said that he was pushing her away because he was trying to spare her. But Mom wouldn't let him off that easy. Dad might have been the troublemaker, but Mom was the fighter. The strongest woman I've ever known. She went through hell and fought the whole way."

I reached for his hand and one corner of his mouth lifted in a tiny smile. I loved when he decided to share things with me. It felt like I got another piece of the puzzle that I never knew I was missing.

Sarah brought out our waters and told us about the different types of drinks.

"We also have some pastries inside. They're made fresh every morning, if you want to take a look."

"Sounds great," I said.

Sarah walked back inside and I had Milo all to myself again. I wanted to lighten the mood, but not at the expense of real and honest conversation. I could talk to him about superficial things all day long. But when he opened up, I wanted to know everything.

"Hollz, is that you?"

I looked away from Milo and saw Colin walking over. We had talked a few times since graduation, but he was spending his free time with Chris and getting ready for college while I was spending all my time with Milo.

"Hey," I said, standing up to hug him. "What are you doing here?"

"Meeting Chris," he said, and then looked between Milo and me. "So you decided to take my advice, huh?"

"I don't think I'll be able to make her leave," Milo said ,and then he shook Colin's hand. "How's it going?"

"Not bad. You?"

"Same."

Colin turned to me and smirked as though Milo was unaware of what he was doing. Subtlety had never been one of Colin's strong suits. When I had initially told him that I was going on a date with Milo, he was more excited about it than I was. After two weeks of spending all our free time together, Colin knew I was falling head over heels, even though I tried to deny it. Meg and Colin knew me better than just about anyone, and were the first to say exactly what was on their minds.

"I'll be right back," Milo said. "I'm gonna check out the pastries inside."

He disappeared through the side door, and Colin took the seat Milo had vacated and rested his arms on the table while he waited for me to speak.

"What?" I asked.

"You know what."

"I do?" I asked, and then changed the subject to our friend. "Have you talked to Meg?"

"Yesterday. Now back to you."

"You're ridiculous."

"I'm ridiculous? Have you told him that you're madly, deeply, hopelessly in love with him?" he asked, and I hit his arm.

"Dude! Stop it," I muttered, looking around to make sure that Milo had missed what Colin had said. "I'm not…whatever it was you just said."

"Yes you are."

"It's barely been two weeks. You're insane."

"Based on what you've told me, what I've heard from Meg, and seeing the two of you together, you can say whatever you want, but you've already fallen for the guy."

"It's too soon," I told him. "Way too soon."

"When did you know that you loved me? Or Meg?"

"I can't remember a time that I didn't love you two."

"So if you can't admit it to me, at least admit it to yourself. You love Milo."

"I love spending time with him. I love the way he makes me laugh. I love kissing him. I *love* all those things. That does not mean that I love him."

"If you say so."

I leaned forward and Colin did the same.

"Okay, yes. I am falling for him. The idea of this summer ending and not being able to spend time with him hurts. If it hurts now, just after a couple of weeks, what's it going to be like in August when I have to go? How am I going to be able to walk away?"

It was the first time I had admitted that out loud, and I felt a piece of my heart break. Feeling for Milo scared me, not because I thought he was not worth it, but because I knew it would crush me in the end.

"Be honest with yourself...and with him. Because the worst thing you could do is deny all those feelings, and kick yourself for not allowing yourself to feel them when you were with him."

"I hate when you're right."

"I know," he said as he stood up.

Colin pulled me to my feet and wrapped his arms around me, hugging me tightly. If I allowed myself to think about August and what it brought with it, I would likely cry. I had done well to avoid those thoughts until Colin forced me.

"You'll be fine," he whispered in my ear. "Even if your heart is broken when it's over, something tells me he will have been worth it. I mean, he waited a long-ass time for you to notice him."

We parted and I looked up at him, not understanding what he meant.

"I did notice him," I said defensively. "He was just too prickly and scary."

Colin laughed and nodded his head behind me. "Yeah, terrifying."

I looked over to see Milo on the ground with Lima and Bean again. He was so happy playing with them, and seeing his smile warmed my heart.

When I looked back at Colin, he smiled and raised a brow. I knew he was prepared to drop more knowledge on me, but he would have to wait because Chris was walking over toward us. We exchanged our hellos and the two of them went inside to get a table. Colin and Chris were relationship goals personified:

supportive, loving, and happy. The things Colin told me, I was sure he had told himself numerous times, because they were going to colleges on opposite sides of the country. And they refused to waste time pretending with each other.

Milo's laughter caught my attention and I looked over at him, knowing exactly how I felt, even if I thought it was too soon.

From the beginning, I had known it would happen. It just surprised me that it had happened so soon.

I had fallen for Milo.

CHAPTER 16

MILO

For a solid month, Holland and I had been dating. Every day that I spent with her made me love her even more—though I never said those words because I was worried that it might scare her away. And every time I was about to say them, I would hear my mom's voice, encouraging me to open up and say what I felt. But I chickened out because those three words were ones I had never said to anyone else besides my mom.

It was early July and our dating bucket list seemed to go by the wayside. A night swim, afternoon with puppies, and a trip to the planetarium seemed to be as far as we got in June. I needed to make the rest of the summer memorable, and I had a few ideas how to make that happen. But the thing about Holland was that she was pretty skittish when it came to most things. The mention of skydiving had her nearly hyperventilating, so I figured maybe we could take baby steps and try one of those simulators. The hard part would be getting her to go along with it.

Holland's dad was in the mood to barbecue—something that

he apparently did often in the summer. I had spent some time with her mom and dad, but her brother and sister had busy lives and were rarely around. When she invited me to swim and hang out at her place after I got off work, I figured we could do our date another day. I would have to find another time, because she really wanted me to hang out with her family.

"What are you working on?" I asked when I walked into her room.

Holland turned around and shut her laptop screen down in a hurry. Between working at the country club, spending most of her free time with me, and getting ready to leave for Westview, I knew she had a lot on her plate.

"Making a list," she said.

"A list?"

"Yeah, things I want to get done before I have to leave."

I peeked over her shoulder, even though the screen wasn't visible. "Am I on that list?" I asked.

"What do you think?" She stood up and faced me with a raised brow.

"Just making sure."

She looked down at my hands and then up at me. "Where are your things?"

"I left them by the front door."

Holland smiled and gave me a quick kiss before taking my hand to lead me outside. The thing that she had failed to mention was that her family included twenty extended family members. We stepped outside and I was shocked to see so many people in the Monroes' back yard. There were people in the pool, others playing darts near the back of the fence, and more sitting around the table on the patio.

"This is my grams," Holland said, walking me to an older woman who was sitting beneath a shade. Her short white hair looked fluffy and barely moved in the wind, but her smile made me at ease.

"Nice to meet you. I'm Milo," I said, shaking her hand.

"Milo. I've heard all about you. Sit down and talk to me," she said, patting the empty chair next to her.

Holland laughed and mouthed that she would be back, leaving me with her grandmother.

"Holland tells me that you want to be an engineer?"

"Yes, ma'am."

"So you must be good with math, huh?"

"I'm pretty good," I admitted. "What about you?"

"I hated math," she laughed. "But I loved science."

"Did you?"

"Yeah, that's probably why I was a good cook. I could measure," she said, cackling at her comment.

"I cook too."

Grams turned in her seat, her mouth slightly agape, and leaned forward. "You cook?"

"Yes, ma'am.'"

She narrowed her eyes and raised her chin like she was thinking, and then grinned. "Grilled cheese doesn't count."

That made me laugh and I agreed with her.

"He's an amazing cook, Grams," Holland said as she joined us.

She placed a glass of water in front of her grandmother and took a seat.

Grams looked between the two of us and nodded. "Did my granddaughter tell you that she brags about you to everyone?"

"Grams," Holland muttered. "Stop it."

"Oh hush," she said with a laugh. "I'm old and I can say things that embarrass you because…I'm old."

"You're not that old," I told her.

"You got a smart one here, honey. Way better than that Blake character I met at Christmas."

Holland looked at me, and her face looked like she had gotten sunburned. I liked that her grandmother did not appear to care for her ex, but I loved that she seemed to really like me.

"You two should go swim or something. It's hot out here. I'll probably go inside and cool off for a little."

"You're not going to swim?" I asked.

"Are you trying to check me out?" Grams teased, and Holland's burst of laughter had her grandmother laughing too.

She helped her grandmother back inside and waved me to follow. Her mom was in the kitchen with some other women who I assumed, based on similar features, were her sisters. I was introduced to Aunt Silvia and Aunt Lisa, both of whom nearly choked me when they hugged me. My mom was an only child and I rarely saw my aunt on my dad's side; being around women was not something I was used to. But Holland's family was kind and inviting.

"If you want, you can leave your stuff in my room," Holland said as we walked down the hallway.

Her room was always clean and orderly, though her mom joked that it was usually a mess.

"Sorry about Grams," she said.

"Are you kidding? She's great."

Holland smiled and wrapped her arms around my waist, holding me tightly. I kissed the top of her head and when she finally let me go, she was staring up into my eyes like there was so much to say but no time to say it. I wanted time alone with her, but between our work schedules and making sure we spent time with our friends, it was increasingly difficult to be together.

"Let's go back outside before Mom comes looking for us," she said.

She gave my hand a tug, but I stayed where I was and pulled her back to me. Holland smiled up at me and I lowered my face, placing my hand to the side of her neck, and kissed her. It was not the kiss I wanted to give her, but considering we were in her parents' house with family all around, it was the only one I could give her at the moment.

When we walked outside, I took my shirt off and walked to the edge of the pool and jumped in. Her little cousins were swimming with floats on their arms and giggled at the waves I had made for them. The tiniest one, a little boy, paddled his way toward me and reached for my hands.

"Hey, buddy," I said. "What's your name?"

"Billy," he said with a bit of a lisp, and then held up his fingers. "I'm three."

"No way! You're three?" I asked exaggeratedly.

Billy nodded his head proudly and then started laughing.

"Who are you?"

When I wasn't looking, Holland jumped into the pool and Billy squirmed away from me to get to his cousin. She picked him up and he wrapped his chubby little arms around her neck.

"Were you just talking to Milo?" she asked Billy.

By this time, the two little girls in the pool, who were a bit older, also swam toward us.

"Holland," one of the girls said. "Is that your *boyfriend*?"

She nodded at them and smiled, causing the two girls to laugh hysterically. Holland playfully splashed water at them, and it caused an all-out splashing war. Everyone in the pool was laughing and screaming as we continued to throw the water around.

"Okay..." Holland shouted. "Truce. Time out."

The girls looked at me and then immediately started kicking their legs in an effort to make sure I stayed drenched.

"Casey and Cammy," Aunt Silvia called out. "Get out of the pool and come eat."

"We don't want to," they whined.

"Now," their mom said sternly.

Holland and I helped the girls out of the pool and Billy decided that he wanted to get out too. I looked at my girlfriend and smiled. She had snuck into the pool when I wasn't paying attention, but I noticed she was wearing the bikini and it made me smile. Everything about her made me smile.

"What are you thinking about?" she asked as she swam toward me.

"You," I laughed. "Always you."

"What about me?"

I looked around at the family that was gathered at her house and shook my head. Holland smirked and rolled her eyes. I followed her to the edge of the pool, where we sat on one of the steps.

"We haven't been doing too good on our bucket list," I said.

"Yeah. I noticed. We kind of suck."

"Not anymore. We're getting back on track."

"We are?"

"So here's the deal: tomorrow, we're going out after work. I made an appointment and I'm not going to tell you anything else about it. You can ask all you want, but I'm not telling."

"I don't like that," she said. "What if I'm scared? What if instead of the lake you take me to the beach where sharks live?"

"But you love the beach," I reminded her.

"Yeah, well, that doesn't mean I'm not afraid of sharks and whatever else is in there."

"What are you, five?" I laughed.

"Shut up," she said, swatting at my arm.

"Do you think that maybe we can sneak away for a little so we can talk?"

Holland turned to face me and cocked her head to the side, her brows pinching together. "That sounds ominous."

"It's not. I swear."

"Should we go now?" she asked.

"If you want. That's fine."

We climbed out of the pool and she handed me a towel before wrapping herself up in one. Her mascara was smudged under her eyes and she was trying to wipe it away, to no avail. I put on my shoes and waited for her to tell her parents that we would be back before slipping out through the side gate.

She was hugging her towel against her body with one hand and fidgeting with her hair with the other. It was not my intention to alarm her, but from the way she avoided eye contact with me, I knew that was what I had done.

There was a tiny park in her neighborhood with a few swings and a slide. Fortunately, when we walked up, no one was there. She walked to one of the swings and sat down, and I took the one next to her. Just as she pushed back to swing, I grabbed ahold of the chain and stopped her mid-glide. The swing wobbled in the air until it came to rest with her staring at me.

I pulled the chain closer to mine and leaned forward so I could kiss her. When we parted, she sighed and closed her eyes before a smile graced her lips.

"Is that what you wanted to talk about?" she asked.

"No."

"Then what?"

I was trying to find the words, but they failed me. I looked at the mulch beneath my feet, and Holland stood up and walked in front of me. She secured the towel that was wrapped around her and stood between my legs, holding on to the chain with both hands.

"What's wrong?"

"I need to tell you something, but I don't know how to say it."

She let go of the chains and tried to take a step back, but I reached out for her and placed my hands on her hips. Slowly I lifted my head up and looked her in the eyes, and it was then that I saw the fear or concern etched in her features.

"Is it too soon to tell you that I love you?" I asked.

Her smile was almost instant as she stepped into my space and lowered herself, placing a kiss against my lips.

She took a step back, her smile brighter than the sun. "I love you too."

"You do?"

"Yeah...I wanted to tell you before, but it just seemed too soon."

"Is it too soon?" I asked.

She shook her head and I stood up, wrapping my arms around her waist, and lifted her off the ground while I kissed her.

"I almost said something when we were in your room, but I didn't want you to think I was trying to get you in bed."

"I wanted to tell you too, but I was scared that it would freak you out," she admitted.

"I don't think there's anything you could do that would freak me out."

CHAPTER 17

HOLLAND

Coming up with a date to surprise Milo took quite a bit of planning. We might have had classes together in high school, but I had never really gotten to know him due to his quiet nature. Of course, since we had been dating I had come to understand the reason for his silence, but it did not explain who he was. I pored over yearbooks, thought back to the rare things he had said and done when we were in class, and even took a chance to go to his house to glance around his room.

Perhaps that was the biggest insight into Milo Davis. I knew he liked engineering and was pretty good at making sketches, but what I did not realize was his love of baseball.

There was a shelf in the corner of his room adorned with trophies, medals, and pictures of teams that he had played on when he was growing up. Upon further snooping, I learned that he had quit playing our junior year, though he never played for our school. His dad mentioned that he enjoyed his club team, but his focus had always been on school.

When my dad got tickets from someone at work to see the Cooperville Ravens, it was my luck that he was unable to use them. It took a bit of convincing for him to hand them over to me, but I was happy when he finally did. I wasn't sure how deep Milo's love of sports was, but who would pass up the chance to sit at the dugout and see the major league team play?

"These seats are awesome," Milo said as we climbed over people to get our spots.

"I know," I squealed.

It made my heart happy that he was excited about the game. When I had parked my car in the closest lot I could find, Milo gushed about what a wonderful girlfriend I was. I loved hearing him sing my praises, and I was even happier that I had managed to pull off a perfect surprise.

"You know there's more," I told him when we sat.

"More?"

"Yep."

I smiled and turned my attention to the field, even though the players were just warming up. He was eager for more information, but I enjoyed a slow torture. After all, he had made me swim at night. In a lake.

"So? Are you gonna tell me?"

"Nope," I laughed, still avoiding eye contact.

He reached over and wrapped his arms around me, kissing my neck as if he thought I was going to cave. I was laughing when a couple of kids walked into our row, calling out to the players on the field. The two little boys were wearing their baseball gloves, holding a white ball in the other hand. Milo and I watched as they eagerly jumped up and down, yelling and screaming for someone, anyone, to come sign their stuff.

"You're not doing it right," Milo said. He leaned forward and started pointing to one of the players who was closest to the dugout. "See that guy? That's Rodrigo. Call him by his name, tell him you're a big fan."

"Okay," one of the boys said with a shrug.

The kids started doing as instructed, catching the attention of number three, Rodrigo Garcia. He waved to the boys and continued warming up. It was all the encouragement they needed before they started calling out to him again, repeating how much they idolized him. The major leaguer threw the ball one last time and started jogging toward the dugout.

"Tell him he's your favorite player," he whispered so the boys would hear.

They nodded, and when Rodrigo was close enough, they repeated what Milo had told them. The baseball player smiled and looked over at my boyfriend with narrowed eyes and pointed at him.

"What? He just pointed at you," I said, barely able to contain my excitement.

Milo said nothing; he just continued to watch as the rookie signed the two baseballs for the kids and talked to them. After a few minutes, Rodrigo turned toward us and lifted his chin before speaking to us.

"How's it goin', Milo?" the baseball player asked.

"Not bad. You?"

Rodrigo looked around and then grinned. "I can't complain."

"You'd be a real asshole if you did," Milo joked.

I could feel my jaw begin to drop as I watched the two engage in light conversation. When I looked over at the two little boys, their wide eyes and open mouths matched how I felt at the moment. Milo was laughing at something Rodrigo had said, and then he stopped suddenly and turned to look at me.

"Ah man, I'm sorry. This is my girlfriend Holland. Holland, this is Rodrigo," he said, as if he was introducing me to any other person.

But Rodrigo Garcia was not just *any* guy. He was the rookie who had signed a deal to play in the majors right out of high school. I knew of him because my dad and Ben were shocked that he had been recruited so young. It was all they had talked about for a week. He had gone to school a couple of towns over. The news stories that came out when he was signed gave hope to all high school boys that they would be recruited, because they all thought they were good enough. Rodrigo Garcia wasn't good—he was amazing.

"Nice to meet you, Holland," Rodrigo said.

"Hi," I managed to say, completely dumbfounded, before I turned to Milo to question him. "How do you know Rodrigo Garcia?"

"Milo and I go way back."

Milo smirked and shrugged his shoulders. "We played together when we were kids. But clearly Rod was a way better player than me."

"Nice touch having the kids play to my ego, by the way," Rodrigo laughed.

"They just wanted to meet their hero," Milo teased.

"Hero? I'm lucky if I get to play an inning."

"But"—I looked between the two of them before focusing on the rookie again—"you hit a homer at your first at bat—in your first pro game."

"I see your girlfriend's a fan," Rodrigo teased.

Milo playfully wrapped an arm around my waist and pretended to pull me away from his friend. Rodrigo laughed and waved to someone in the dugout who threw him a baseball. He grabbed a pen and started writing on the ball before tossing it to me, but Milo caught it instead. When he looked at what was written, he started laughing and then handed the ball to me.

"Don't you have a game to play?"

The baseball player looked at the field, where several of his teammates were starting to walk back to the dugout after warming up.

"I'm sure they'll give me hell later," he said, hitching a thumb at the guys behind him. "They'll get over it."

"I can't believe you two know each other," I said, finally able to find my voice.

Rodrigo smiled and nodded, but someone in the box was talking to him. "Looks like I gotta go, but it was good seeing you, man. We need to catch up."

"Sounds good. Let's do that when you're not traveling...so Christmas?" Milo said with a laugh.

"Yeah, I got your number. I'll call you." Rodrigo looked up at me once more and smiled. "It was nice meeting you, Holland."

"You too," I managed to say as he disappeared beneath the dugout ceiling.

I looked at the baseball to read what the guy had written, and found my cheeks burning.

I think he likes you. ~#3 R. Garcia

"The things I don't know about you," I sighed.

"But isn't it fun learning?" he asked before kissing my cheek.

That it was. There was no denying that I had completely fallen for Milo Davis. But there was also no denying that with each passing day, I dreaded what would be our fate when I left for Westview. He had become such a staple in my life, and to be without him felt almost as hard as letting go of Meg when she had left.

"You okay?" Milo asked.

I choked out a response that I was fine, though I was sure he did not really buy it. I was barely able to focus on the first half of the game. One moment I was watching a play, and the next I would be lost in a sea of thoughts of everything I would miss about Milo. We still had nearly two months together, but all I could see was the end. I knew that was not the way to spend my time with him, but that day it weighed heavily on me.

"Ladies and gentlemen, please turn your attention to the screen. Get those lips ready, it's time for the kiss cam!" a booming voice announced in the stadium.

I heard the roaring laughter at the couple who appeared on the screen, so I looked up and just as the camera landed on a young couple. Both were shaking their heads furiously, leaning to opposite sides to avoid kissing.

"C'mon, let's have a kiss," the voice pushed.

Both of them continued to shake their heads, and the girl was mouthing something. I leaned forward and squinted my eyes to make out what she was saying and then started laughing.

"What?" Milo asked, trying to figure it out.

"That's her brother!"

"That's messed up," Milo laughed.

"So bad," I agreed.

The camera eventually moved on to find another victim, landing on an older couple who were more than willing to show their love. Seeing them make out made me squeamish because the display was overkill. The audience cheered them on, and I started laughing and buried my head into Milo's shoulder.

"Tell me when it's over," I pleaded.

The crowd continued to laugh and applaud as the camera tried to find more willing participants. And then it happened. Milo tapped my shoulder.

"It's over," he said.

"Oh thank God," I muttered, sitting up again. "That was cringeworthy."

"Hey babe," Milo said.

When I looked up at him, he grinned and pointed to the screen. It was there I saw the two us, larger than life, our faces emblazoned on the big screen. My face turned the brightest shade of red and I looked at him, my nervous laughter the only thing to keep me from dying of humiliation.

"Just kiss me," he said. "Give the people what they want."

I was still laughing and shook my head, which the announcer took as rejection.

"Just one little smooch," the voice said.

I rolled my eyes and smiled up at Milo.

"If you wanted to kiss me, all you had to do was ask," I said.

He gently cradled my cheek in his hand, the way he often did, and placed a simple, chaste kiss to my lips. The crowd cheered and then our faces disappeared from the screen, allowing me to kiss him once more—because I wanted to.

"Did you plan that?" I asked.

"How could I? I didn't even know we were coming here."

"True."

"Maybe you planned it," he said.

"You know me—anything to get you to show me how you feel," I joked.

He had managed to distract me from my thoughts of our impending fate so I was focused on the game. And him. We spend the final innings cheering on the Ravens, who went on to win the game five to three. When the game ended, people were clearing the stadium and Milo started to stand up so we could leave.

"We're not done," I told him.

"We're not?"

"My surprise is definitely not as cool as finding out you know Rodrigo Garcia, but I do have something else planned."

"And that is?"

"We get to walk onto the field," I told him.

"Really?"

"Yeah. It was part of the deal with these tickets my dad got. We just have to wait until they tell us we can go."

"You're pretty awesome."

His compliment was sweet, but all I had done was get the tickets from my dad. It was not nearly as romantic as his night swim idea, or even our first date, but I was glad he liked it. While we were waiting for the attendants to come get us, I turned in my seat to get a better view of his face and lifted my hand to his face, touching the scar I had noticed so many times before.

"How did you get this?" I asked.

"I got into a fight in third grade and the other kid punched me in the eye."

"What? Are you serious?"

"No," he said with a burst of laughter, and I slapped his arm

148

playfully. "I tripped and fell when I was a kid. Got stitches and apparently screamed bloody murder the whole time."

"You're awful," I said.

"Yeah, but you love me anyway."

"I guess," I answered noncommittally.

Before he could respond, an older gentleman walked over and asked us to follow him to the side gate. Milo took my hand in his and we walked together to an entrance that allowed us on the field. The ground felt soft as we stepped out, and I looked up at the enormity of the stadium.

"You have thirty minutes," the man said as he closed the gate and took a seat.

I took off running and Milo chased after me as I laughed. Adrenaline coursed through my veins as I made the effort to stay ahead of him, but he was fast. My feet slowed as I reached first base, and he approached and then ran past me to second. We continued running until we reached home plate, sprinting to the finish. We were breathing heavily as we stood face to face, laughing and arguing about who touched the plate first.

"It was me," I argued, taking a deep breath in an effort to slow my racing heart.

"Fine, first to the pitcher's mound wins," he said. "Are you ready?"

I got into a running stance and he did the same before counting off to three. But just before he said three, I took off running with him once again trailing me. When my feet reached the mound, I jumped up and down triumphantly just as he reached me and wrapped his arms around my waist, hoisting me into the air. He spun me around and set me to my feet, looking down at me so sweetly.

"This was the best. Thank you," he said.

I smiled at him. "I'm glad you liked it."

"I loved it," he said, and then quickly added, "And I love you."

I didn't need to respond because he already knew how I felt.

So instead of telling him, I pushed up on my toes kissed him, pouring everything I could into it. I was afraid that if I had to speak, I would ruin a perfect day by telling him how sad I was that our time was limited, so I did the only thing I could: I showed him.

CHAPTER 18

HOLLAND

Milo and I had one mutual friend, and that was Ethan. I had had classes with him over the years, and the one thing I loved about the guy was his unabashed way of making everyone laugh and feel like they were old friends. There were few people that I could name who did not love the guy—myself included.

Ethan and Milo grew up living next door to each other, and by all accounts, knew the other better than either would like to admit. They likely had secrets that rivaled the ones that Meg and I shared, though Milo often downplayed their bond. That is until Ethan texted an emoji of a dart gun along with a time and location.

"What does that mean?" I asked, looking over his shoulder at the text that made Milo smile and scoff.

"It's just this thing…It's nothing," he said as he typed a response.

Milo: Sorry. Busy with Holland.

"What? Don't blame me," I said quickly. "What are you blaming me for?"

"It's just a stupid thing we do every year. It's no big deal."

"You do it every year and it's no big deal?"

He cocked his head to each side, cracking his neck, and then smiled shyly. That was another smile that I liked on him. I had started to learn what each smile meant, and the one he wore at that moment was my favorite.

"When we were about seven, his dad bought him a Nerf gun. And since neither of us were particularly good at sharing, my dad got me one too. As soon as I opened mine, we started having a war. We would run all over the place and hide until we got the other."

"That sounds like fun," I laughed. "But you only played once a year?"

"No, that's the thing…we played all the time."

"So what's so special about this particular time?"

"He came to my house one day, before we all had phones, and said that he was challenging me to a battle to end all battles…the big one, he called it. And I grabbed my gear and we went after each other like it was the real thing. And it was fun."

"I guess so, if you do it every year."

Milo smiled and grew more excited as he continued to talk about it.

"The next year it was me who challenged him, and it's gone back and forth ever since. We spend one afternoon acting like jackasses, and then we grab some food and hang out after."

"And today's the day," I said, not questioning it.

"Well, it can be any day. The person who challenges can select the time and day, but it's not exactly a year to the day."

"Milo, you *have* to do this," I said, excited for him.

Milo's phone buzzed again and he looked down to read his message. The smile, which still had not faded as he had told me the story, only grew when he turned the screen to face me.

Ethan: Bring her.

"Oh hell yeah," I said, standing up. "Where do we go?"

Milo stood up and raised a brow curiously. It was nice that I could surprise him with things I said and did. And apparently agreeing to partake in a silly childhood game was surprising to him.

"You want to go?" he asked.

"Ethan just invited me to—you bet I'm going."

"Damn, you're awesome," he said.

He walked over to his closet and I watched as he dug around, throwing a few things out on the floor behind him. I would have offered to help if I had known what he was searching for in there. And then there was the sound of victory, a loud *yes* that was followed by my boyfriend turning to look at me with the weapon in hand.

"That's it?" I asked, looking at the one toy gun in his hand.

Milo laughed and shook his head. "This one is for you."

He walked over to the footlocker that was at the end of his bed and opened it up. Inside was a treasure trove of spongy darts and launching items. He pulled out one that looked like a water gun and held it up to show me.

"This is Baby."

"Baby?"

His lopsided smile was adorable as he went on to explain. "This thing can hold a hundred rounds. I've been waiting for this call so I can use it on Ethan."

"What if he has one too?"

"I assume he does, and that's why he's challenging me now."

"This is the cheesiest, most awesome thing, I've ever heard of. But...with all that stuff you have there, why do I get the crappy little gun with three darts?"

"You have to work your way up to the big guns," he teased.

I fired off one shot and hit his arm while he looked at me in shock. I started laughing and aimed, prepared to fire another round at him.

"I think I just worked my way up. I need a better gun. Don't hold out on me."

Milo looked at the gun in my hand then looked at the one in his. I could tell he was contemplating hitting me with the small rubber pellet, but thought better of it. His goal was to unload them on Ethan; it would be wasted on me.

"Fine," he said. "I'll let you use Betty."

"Betty? Do you name all of your Nerf guns?"

"Well...yeah."

"You're such a dork...I love you," I laughed.

"Let's get going and I'll tell you the rules on the way."

"On the way? But Ethan lives right next door."

"We're not doing it here," Milo said.

We drove about twenty minutes to the lake where Milo had taken me on our second date. It brought back memories of that night, and by the way he was looking at me, I knew he was thinking the same thing.

The whole drive, he had gone over how the game worked— which was pretty much that anything went. The first one to run out of ammunition was the loser, and considering I had about twenty darts, I would likely be the first casualty.

When we got out of the car, we walked to the beach area where a few people were sunbathing. They were too busy enjoying the beautiful July day to be bothered by us. Ethan walked toward us with a grin on his face as he carried his version of Baby in his arms. He immediately noticed the one in Milo's hands and his smiled wavered slightly.

"I hope you don't mind, but I invited some others to the game," Ethan said, pointing over our shoulders.

I turned around and noticed that Daryl and Hunter were approaching with their own weapons, and I started to laugh nervously.

"This is not going to end well," I said quietly, so only Milo could hear. "Maybe I should just watch."

"I don't think you're the watch-and-see type," he answered. "Besides, now you get to be on my team."

"Oh no…" Hunter scoffed. "You don't get to have her on your team."

"What? Why not?" Milo asked.

"It's a rule I just made up," Hunter said.

"Whose team am I on?" I asked.

"It's every man…or woman…for themselves," Daryl said.

"Fine," Milo said. "Then let's do this."

"Wait. Not everyone is here," Ethan said. "We can't start yet."

"Who are we waiting on?"

Before Ethan could answer, Alice jogged toward us, calling out her apologies. She was one of the star volleyball players we went to school with and at five foot ten, her height was no match for Ethan's six-foot frame. She was one of the nicest girls ever, and the idea of her playing in a harmless Nerf war seemed a stretch, but there she was anyway.

I turned to Ethan and grinned. "When did this happen?"

His smile was shy and he shrugged. "First date."

Milo closed his eyes and shook his head as he started to laugh. It took me a moment to catch up, but I realized the reason for the impromptu challenge was less about the game and more about easing the first-date tension.

"I'm sorry I'm late," Alice repeated when she was close enough. "I had to bribe my little brother to let me borrow his stuff."

"You're fine," Ethan said. "We haven't even started yet."

Alice smiled and said her hellos to all of us before Milo and Ethan told the four of us the rules. I knew that most of the rules were probably bendable, because they had been playing the game for so long and it was all in good fun.

When the time came for the game to start, we stood in a circle, all six of us with our backs to the center. When they counted to ten, we had to run and find a spot to use as our hideout until we were ready to capture someone.

"Ten," they shouted, and I took off running for the largest tree I could find.

One would think I would have turned to see where everyone else went, but I was so focused on finding my hiding spot.

My heart was pounding and I tried to keep from laughing until I heard the bushes behind me rustling. Slowly I turned around, fearing a snake or some other wild creature, only to find Hunter aiming his fake gun at me. I pulled my own trigger and shot two at him, which only made him laugh.

"Careful, Hollz...you're down two shots now."

"Damn it," I muttered.

He took off running and I chanced a look around the tree to see if anyone was visible, and the only person I saw was Alice. When I fired, my dart missed her, but she screamed with laughter and ran off to hide again.

"Get it together," I said to myself quietly.

I spotted Ethan running from one tree to another and waited

for my chance to strike. He was looking around, careful not to make too much noise, and then I heard his laugh as he fired at Daryl. I quickly fired off a round at Ethan.

"Ah, damn," he said, not stopping to see who had gotten him.

I stifled a laugh and tucked myself further behind the tree so as to go unnoticed when there was another crackling sound behind me.

"I got ya," I heard Milo say.

I turned around, ready to defend myself, but his hand was at his side, the Nerf gun slung over his shoulder. I smiled as he walked in my direction, stopping to quickly kiss me.

"I won't let them get you," he said before winking at me. "Ethan is a good shot, but Daryl...he'll fire his rounds about five times just hoping to get you once. Don't shoot at him. He'll run out of ammunition before anyone else."

I showed him the piece in my hand and scoffed. "Doubt it. I wasted three already."

"Don't get trigger-happy. You have to be strategic."

"Okay. I'll try."

He kissed me again and smiled. "Are you having fun?"

"So much fun," I laughed. "This is an awesome date."

"This counts as a date?" he asked. "Score for me."

I pushed at his chest lightly and waved him off. "Go play, or I'm going to shoot at you."

"No you won't, because I'm the only one who's looking after you." He grinned.

"Yeah, well you and Ethan have a lot of pellets in those things."

We could hear the laughter and yelps from the others as they continued to capture each other. We had only been playing for about ten minutes, and I still had the majority of my darts, and another sleeve that Milo had attached to a sash across my chest.

Milo started to leave but stopped when he heard the trees shaking behind us. I knew someone was about to tag both of us, but to our surprise it was all four of them, surrounding us.

"What's going on?" Milo asked with a nervous laugh.

Ethan shrugged his shoulders and grinned, taking a step forward. Milo moved to stand in front of me and Ethan chuckled.

"This is too easy."

Milo turned his face toward me and muttered, "Run."

"What?" I asked.

"Run!" he called out as Ethan began to fire at us.

I took off running like I was told as he followed me. I could hear the shouts of the others as they ran behind us, and I stopped running only to fire off my remaining rounds at them.

"What are you doing?" Milo asked.

"Run. Go hide so you can win," I said as I continued to hit them.

Milo ran and Ethan followed as I unloaded all of my darts on Daryl, Hunter, and Alice. The three of them starting firing at each other and soon all of us were empty and ready to do something else.

I grabbed the cooler from the trunk of Milo's car and we hung out and snacked while he and Ethan continued chasing each other. It took them some time to finish off their game, but when they did, they walked over to join us, laughing as they high-fived their childish antics that the rest of us thoroughly enjoyed.

Milo sat down next to me and kissed me once before grabbing a water bottle and chugging it down. Alice cozied up next to Ethan, and he was more than happy with the attention. Unfortunately, the heat was beginning to take its toll on us, so the six of us jumped into the lake to cool down.

I swam toward Milo, who was standing in waist-deep water, waiting for me to reach him. I stood up and wrapped my arms around his neck and hugged him tightly. The day had been one that I needed, and he was the reason for that.

"Thanks for being so cool," he whispered in my ear.

"Thanks for being so you," I said. "This was fun."

"Well, next time it's just you and me."

"That sounds good too," I said.

CHAPTER 19

HOLLAND

"So how are things with you and Milo?" Meg asked.

Her classes kept her busier than either of us had expected, and the planned phone calls to connect often ended within a few short minutes because of work or her need to study. I missed her so much and I missed all the things we planned to do together.

"They're really good," I answered. "How's school?"

"Hell. Remind me to never do this again," she said with an exasperated sigh. "This psych class is killing me."

"I'm sorry," I muttered. "How much longer do you have?"

"Another week. I'm really looking forward to the time off. Get some of my summer back."

"Wait. What? I thought you had classes for both sessions."

"I did, but this one was so fast and stressful, I decided to take a break."

"Does this mean you're coming home?" I asked optimistically.

She was quiet as I waited for an answer, but her silence told me everything I already knew. It was ridiculous how I got my hopes up in mere moments, because disappointment would follow.

"I think I need to stay here and adjust. Figure everything out before the fall starts."

"Yeah…I understand," I said, trying to sound as supportive and upbeat as I could. "Makes sense."

"Besides, you have Milo and your bucket list…How's that coming?"

"We hit a bit of a pause. Our schedules have been so opposite and one or both of us has been too tired for anything more than takeout and a movie."

"Oh, that's no good," she said. "You need to fix that."

"Actually…I did. I got tickets from Dad and we went to see the Ravens play the other day. It was awesome. But you want to know the crazy part? Remember the rookie, Rodrigo?"

"Garcia? Sexy as hell? Yes, I remember. Go on."

"Milo knows him! Can you believe that?"

"No…way!"

"Yeah, he introduced me him and he's super nice."

"Nice? Who cares about that? What does he look like up close?" she asked eagerly.

"He's cute."

"Cu…I hate coupled Holland…She doesn't give details like single Holland."

"Sorry," I said. "That's about all I can say."

"Fine. So what's the next date? Y'all need to stick to it."

"I agree. I mean, the things we *have* done have been pretty great."

"So keep it up."

"Yeah…" I trailed off, allowing myself to go into that dark space.

"Don't do it."

"Do what?"

"I know what you're thinking about right now, and you have to stop. You still have almost two months left together until you leave."

"I hate that you know me so well," I groaned.

"No you don't, because if you didn't have me, you'd be lost."

No truer words were ever spoken by Meg. She had been my other half for so long that sometimes I thought she knew me better than I knew myself. I needed her to remind me to be in the present.

"Okay, fine. Now what about you? Have you heard from Knox since you left?"

"We've texted a few times, but we knew that nothing was going to happen. I mean, sure, it would've been nice, but totally impractical."

"I know...that's what I'm afraid of."

"But you and Milo are different. Knox and I had a date. You're in a relationship, with all that entails. You could be tired of each other come August," she said lightheartedly.

"I seriously doubt that."

"Yeah, that's what I thought. You're probably trying to work up the courage to say the L word."

When I remained quiet, Meg must have taken my silence for an admission of sorts, which I guess it was. I heard her gasp and I knew I was about to be pummeled with more questions.

"You told him you love him?"

"Actually, it was Milo."

"No way. But...isn't it kinda too soon?"

"I can't explain it, Meg. He makes me so happy. When I'm around him, I feel like we're in our own little world and there is no concept of time. I'm completely in love with Milo, and it scares me because I know that I'm leaving and it hurts my heart to even think about that."

"Then don't. We're not going to talk about August or when you leave. From now on, we're just going to focus on the here and now."

"I wish I could flip that switch in my head. You know, there are some days that I want to break it off. Not because I don't love him, but to make it easier for when I do have to leave. But then I see his face and all I want to do is be in his arms for as long as I can."

"Then that's what you need to do. Be with Milo. Enjoy your time. And worry about the rest when it happens."

160

"Damn, I miss you. I wish you were home."

"No you don't," she laughed. "Because then you'd be dividing your time between me and Milo and going crazy in the process."

"Again, you're right."

"Two words I never tire of hearing," she sighed happily.

I looked at the clock and knew if I waited much longer, I would be late for work. We said our goodbyes and I grabbed my things before walking to the kitchen to grab some water. Dad was sitting at the breakfast table looking at his tablet, but put it down when he saw me.

"How's it goin', honey?"

"Good. About to go to work. Just got off the phone with Meg."

"How's she doing?"

"She sounds great. I miss her like crazy, but she sounds pretty good."

"You should plan a trip to visit her, I bet she'd enjoy that."

"You're probably right. But…"

"I know, you don't want to leave the boyfriend," he chuckled, raising his hands in mock surrender. "It was just a suggestion."

"And one I might really consider. But right now, I have to get to work. I'm going out with Milo after, so I might be home late. But I'll keep you and Mom posted."

"All right, have a good day."

I kissed his cheek and rushed out the door. It was not my best idea, but I ignored the posted speed signs on my way to work. Hendricks had been on a rampage about people showing up late and skipping out early from their shifts. I was always early and stayed well past my time, but I knew the one time I showed up late, she would probably shred me about it. My goal for work, aside from avoiding Brandon—stay on Hendricks' good side.

It took about fifteen minutes to get to the country club, and I made it with seconds to spare. Hendricks looked up at the clock as I strolled in but went back to staring at her phone. I put on my apron and clocked in before checking with Daphne about my section.

After the incident with Brandon, Daphne had done a good job

of keeping him and Milo out of each other's way. I, on the other hand, still worked with him more than I would like. He managed to keep the inappropriate comments to a minimum, though I still hated when we shared sections. It was as if he was trying to make sure Milo noticed that we were working near each other.

But Milo was so secure with our relationship that he barely paid any attention to Brandon. He chose instead to focus his spare time talking with me or checking me out when he thought I wasn't looking.

I had heard rumors that Brandon was seeing someone and he had been much less attentive to me, which I appreciated.

That morning, Milo was scheduled to come in a little later than I was because he had some things to take care of at home. When I asked about it, he had said he and his dad were meeting with someone who was going to work on the patio that needed some repair. It seemed a little strange to me, because their deck was perfectly fine, but I chose not to question it because it was none of my business.

It was nearly eleven in the morning before Milo showed up, and when he walked through the back door I caught his eye and smiled. He looked distracted until he noticed me, and I was rewarded with my favorite smile—the one that showed off the dimples in his cheeks. He gave me a wink and then walked over to Jaysen and Carlo, who were busy cooking, as usual.

I was distractedly watching him while he started to cut the vegetables for a dish they were preparing. He was methodical with every slice, and I knew that cooking was not just a means to an end. He was good at it because he loved it.

"Holland," Brandon called out gruffly, snapping me out of my mental break, "table nineteen is asking for you."

"Okay. I'll be right there."

Brandon walked out through the kitchen doors into the main dining area. I walked toward Milo, and when no one was looking I gave him a quick kiss on the cheek.

"I can't wait to get off work," I said.

"Me too…and I just got here."

When I walked into the main dining area, the older couple that I had been waiting on waved me over and requested their check. Mr. and Mrs. Ramirez were regulars at Pine Bridge who often requested to sit in my section. I think they liked that I listened to their stories about how the club used to be when they were younger. Others who waited on them would listen for a moment and find an excuse to get away. But I enjoyed visiting with them.

"Here you are, honey," Mrs. Ramirez said, handing me the tablet with her credit card.

I started to walk away, but she placed a gentle hand on my forearm.

"Was there something else?" I asked.

"I thought I saw you the other day in town—with a rather handsome-looking young man."

When I was embarrassed, my cheeks always gave me away, and Mrs. Ramirez picked up on my tell. I started to smile and she patted my arm before looking at her husband.

"I told you it was her."

"Leave her alone, Esther. Can't you see you're embarrassing the girl?"

"It's fine," I said. "I'll be right back."

I walked to the kiosk and charged her credit card while trying to get my face to return to its normal beige shade. Without his saying a word, I knew Brandon was standing right behind me. He huffed loudly and cleared his throat, but the machine was running slow for some reason.

"Sorry, just give me a second."

"Don't rush on my account…The view isn't too bad from here."

I spun around to tell him off and he was closer than I expected. When I looked around the restaurant, there were too many people around and I refused to make a scene and risk my tips.

"That's enough," I warned through clenched teeth.

"I'm just joking," he said with a smirk. "Just trying to lighten the mood around here. You've been so tense since you started dating the kitchen boy."

163

"Milo."

"Milo…whatever. Not like it's gonna last anyway."

"What would you know?"

"Please," he huffed. "You're leaving in a month. You really think you're going to want to be with some kitchen—"

"Watch it," I warned.

"—guy," he finished. "When you'll be off meeting other likeminded people?"

"Brandon, you know nothing about Milo, me, or our relationship."

"I know more than you think," he said snidely as he pointed at the kiosk. "You're done."

I turned around and grabbed the receipt before tucking it inside the black folder I stashed in my apron. Brandon was still standing uncomfortably close as I shoved past him. I took a deep breath and calmed my frayed nerves, pasting on my most convincing smile.

"Here you go."

I placed the check presenter on the table and asked if they needed anything else before I walked away. They stood up to leave and Mrs. Ramirez gave me a tender hug.

"Your fella is much better than that one," she said. "He has trouble written all over him."

She looked behind me and I knew she was talking about Brandon. All I could do was smile, and it was no longer forced because I wholeheartedly agreed with her. Mr. Ramirez took her hand in his and they walked out together. I was happy with Milo, and validation on our relationship was not something I sought from others, but it was nice that she could see how good Milo was for me.

Still, Brandon's warning and my own fears were heavy on my mind. And then Meg's wise words came to me, reminding me to be in the present with Milo. I would make sure I enjoyed every second we had together because I refused to live with regrets when it came to us.

***

The rest of my shift went on without another incident with

Brandon. Thankfully, I made great tips and was ready for whatever Milo had planned for our afternoon. I followed him to his house in my car so we could get ready for this mystery date that he had arranged for us.

After the night swim, when it came to his dates for us, I was always a little more than hesitant because it was clear he liked to take chances that were a little harder for me. Still, I would coax myself to relax and go with the flow because he would never let me get hurt.

I was wearing a pair of denim shorts and a white tank with a button-down shirt over it. It had been a particularly warm day, and the moment I walked onto the patio to sit with him, I was covered in sweat. Milo opened up his laptop and turned the screen to face me. He was smiling so beautifully it was hard not to return the smile. I hit the button on the screen so I could see what made him so happy.

The heat outside was nothing compared to the fear-inducing sweat that was happening in my pits as I watched the video. People being lifted from the floor, horizontal as they floated in the air. Sure, they looked happy, but clearly those people were just insane.

"I'll be right back," he said before disappearing inside the house.

I continued to watch the videos, not feeling any more comforted with each display. There was something unnatural about not having your feet planted firmly on the ground. I knew he would be disappointed that I was too scared to go along, but I was well aware of my limits. And that one—it was just too much for me to take.

With laptop in hand, I walked inside his house and found him in his room, stuffing things into a bag.

"I need to tell you something," I said.

He stopped moving and sat down at his desk as I handed him the computer.

"I can't do this," I muttered under my breath as I sat on the edge of his bed. I could feel all the life leave my body just at the thought of the simulator.

"Do what?" he asked timidly, his features completely frozen in a state of fear or shock, I could not tell which.

He moved away from the desk and wheeled his chair to where I was sitting, his knees pressed gently against mine. I sat still, staring at my hands as I continued to fidget with them nervously. Slowly he reached out a hand and placed it over mine that stilled as soon as he touched me.

"Hollz, what are you saying?" he asked again.

When I lifted my face to look at him, I nodded my head toward the computer screen and shook my head.

"I'm too scared. I can't do real skydive, let alone an indoor simulator."

Milo exhaled loudly and glanced at the floor, shaking his head. Soon his shoulders were shaking, and when he looked up at me, he did not even try to contain his laughter.

"Shut up," I said, trying to pull my hands away, but he held on a little tighter. "You're mean."

"I'm sorry," he said through his laughter. "But you scared me."

"Are you kidding me? You want me to skydive and *I'm* scaring you?"

"First off…it's a simulator. It's awesome. But that's not what I'm laughing at. I thought you were trying to break up with me or something."

"What? Are you crazy? Why in the world would I break up with you?"

"Exactly, because I'm the perfect boyfriend."

"Eh," I said with a shrug. "You're all right."

"All right?"

"Yeah. So-so."

"So-so?"

"I mean, I guess as far as boyfriends go, you're okay."

"Okay?"

"Are you just going to keep repeating everything I say?"

"Everything you say?"

"Ack! You're hopeless," I laughed.

"Now that, I absolutely agree with," he said as he playfully lunged toward me.

I fell back on the bed, laughing hysterically as he lay next to me, tickling my side. No matter how much I squirmed, he managed to find the exact spot that had me rolling in laughter.

"Okay. Okay…stop," I said, breathless.

Milo stopped and I looked up at him as he propped his head on his hand, staring down at me with that smile. I touched the little scar on his eye and he took my hand in his. As he brought my hand to his lips, he kissed it once and then stared down at me.

"You know I'd never make you do anything you don't want to do," he said with such sincerity.

"I know."

"Good. Because I love you and I would never intentionally hurt you."

"I know that too."

"Okay, so what else do you know…since you apparently know everything?" he asked.

With my available hand, I reached up and held his face, pulling his lips to mine. Just before our lips met, I smiled.

"I love you too."

The tinge of mint lingered in the space between his lips and mine. Neither of us moved to close it but the air was heavy with fears unspoken and feelings bigger than either of us imagined. It felt like an eternity before he lowered his face, his lips grazing against mine. As our mouths began the dance they had mastered when we first started dating, something else shifted between us.

Milo's hand trailed from my neck to my waist, where he gently caressed my side. I wrapped both of my arms around his neck as he deepened the kiss, his tongue tangling with mine. Milo moved, bearing his weight on his arms as he hovered over me. I pulled him against me; the weight of his body on mine offered a blanket of warmth that minutes before would have felt suffocating.

Uncertainty and longing were feuding inside of me as the warmth of his hand trailed across my exposed stomach. We had never talked about taking the next step, but every time I was with him it was harder and harder to stop. Being with Milo—holding him—felt so right. I knew that we loved each other, but the timing didn't feel right. And every time we ended up in that position, as much as I wanted to be with him, I couldn't go through with it. Milo was always so patient and sweet when I pushed pause, though I know we both wanted more.

"Hey, Mi," his dad called out as the door shut behind him. "I'm home."

I practically shoved Milo off of me and he fell to the floor with a loud thud. He looked up at me, a disheveled mess, and started laughing. In an attempt to hide my guilt, I sat up and tried to smooth down my hair, but if he was any indication, it was obvious what had been happening between us.

When I glared at him and tried to shush him, it only made him laugh more. He got to his feet and reached for my hand.

"Don't worry, you don't look like you just tried to attack me," he said before kissing me chastely.

I slapped his arm and held his hand as we walked into the living room where his dad was just sitting down on the couch.

"Hey there, Holland." Mr. Davis smiled. "I didn't know you were here."

"We were supposed to go out," Milo said. "But she doesn't want to go."

"I don't blame ya," he said. "It's hot out there."

I nodded, but kept my mouth shut because the only response that I had for him needed to stay tucked in my head.

Not as hot as it was in here.

CHAPTER 20

MILO

After Holland went home, I was alone in my room, lying on the spot where we had been making out earlier. I had never wanted someone as much as I wanted her. Each time we ended up in a compromising position where there was little to stop us, something would happen to douse it with a bucket of cold water—like Dad getting home earlier than expected. Holland had looked both relieved and disappointed at the sound of his voice. I wasn't lying before when I had told her I would never hurt her, and I hoped she understood that also meant when it came to sex.

"Got a sec?" Dad asked when he walked into my room.

"Yeah," I said, sitting upright. "What's up?"

"We need to have a talk."

"Is everything okay?"

"Well, you have to tell me."

"Yeah, everything's fine," I said, though it sounded like a question because I was not sure what he was talking about.

169

"Is Holland okay?"

"Yeah…why?"

"Son, I'm not stupid. I know what was going on when I got home."

"What are you talking about? Nothing was going on. We were playing a video game," I lied, unconvincingly, which only made me sound guilty.

Dad sat down on the edge of my bed, but remained quiet. We failed at the meaningful talks—always had. Mom was the one who kept the conversations going, and when she had died, it was hard to breach the gap left by her absence. We tried to listen to each other, but it was tough because we were too much alike.

"Okay. So…did she want to play *video games*?" he asked, emphasizing the word.

Shit. Is this the *talk?*

I cleared my throat and tried to look him in the eye, but then took a deep breath and focused my attention to the picture of Holland and me that was on my desk. Her mom had given it to me a few days after the barbeque party at their house. She had taken it when we returned from the park, after I had told her I loved her.

"Nothing happened," I finally admitted, which had my dad exhaling loudly.

"I'm not going to have the talk with you. I think you know all the mechanics and the safe sex talk," he said, which made me cringe. "But I am going to have a different talk with you."

"What's that?"

"Respect."

I turned and looked at Dad, offended at the single word he uttered.

"I love her. Of course I respect her."

"I know you do. But you have to make sure that you listen to her, Mi."

"I do."

"No. I mean *listen* to her. No means no."

"I know that, Dad."

"Son, I don't care how far you've gotten—if she says no, you stop. It's as much for her protection as it is for yours. You have to be careful. Respect her boundaries and listen to her. You got it?" There was an edge to his tone when he finished speaking.

"Yeah, Dad," I muttered. "I got it. But you know I'd never do anything to hurt her."

"I know that. But sometimes women change their minds…and that's okay. She's allowed to change her mind."

I nodded and Dad, seemingly satisfied that we had had his version of the talk, stood up to leave my room. As he reached the doorway, he paused and looked over his shoulder at me and waited for me to give him my attention.

"Make sure that she wants to…*play the video game too*…and you can always just pause it until you're both ready."

I smiled at his metaphor and he left the room, content that he had satisfied his parental duty. I appreciated the effort, as painfully awkward as it was, but it was unnecessary. There was no rush to have sex, and given that she would be leaving in a month, I doubted she was ready for anything more to happen between us.

We had enough on our plate with her impending move to Westview, and I was certain she didn't want to confuse the issue with sex. Besides, the list we had for memorable dates had become boring and stereotypical. I wanted to do something that would make her smile.

It was hard to come up with dates that Holland was interested in. She had dated Blake for several months, and I was certain he had managed to keep her attention because she was always happy when she was with him. I needed to up my game, and I thought the sky-diving simulator was the perfect answer. But she nearly broke out in hives just watching the video. Her response made me rethink the other ideas I had for the two of us.

Cliff-diving at Deer Lake was something I had always wanted to do, but I had a feeling that Holland would not fare too well in that situation. Then I considered taking her hiking in the forest, but what if that was too much for her too?

Instead, I thought back on the things I knew of her from high school, hoping that something might interest her.

171

It was strange to think that for so long I had liked Holland based on how she was in our classes, though she had never seemed to pay much attention to me. The reality that somehow I had gotten her to agree to a date was not lost on me. She was so much more than just the sexy girl in my class. She was smart, and goofy as hell. Anytime we were together, I found myself hoping that the summer dragged on longer so I could spend more time with her.

And I was not the only one to see all the awesome things about Holland Monroe. Luckily for me, she was not interested in any of the other guys.

***

It was Thursday night and we were both off until Saturday, but it was a request I had asked of Daphne a week earlier when she was working on the schedule. I needed some time to make our latest bucket list date go off without a hitch—but that meant that I would have to do the one thing I hated. But for her, I would do it.

I would dance.

"Where are we going?" Holland asked as I drove out of town.

I looked over and smiled. "Don't worry, your feet will stay firmly planted on the ground...well, for the most part."

"Milo," she groaned as she grew more anxious. "You're making me nervous."

"Don't be nervous," I said, reaching for her hand and threading her fingers with mine.

Her knee was bobbing up and down repetitively as she nervously worried her bottom lip. I could tell that with every passing mile she was trying to determine if there was a hint somewhere that she could figure it out. What she failed to understand was that I knew how her brain worked, which was why I had booked the lesson out of Pine Bridge.

"We're almost there," I told her.

She kept a tight grip on my hand as we made our way to the nondescript building, only letting go when I had to park my car. As she stepped out, I took the opportunity to stare at her again. When I had gotten to her house, I was blown away by how beautiful she looked in her simple black fitted dress with her hair down. I was so

172

used to the ponytail that anytime she changed even the slightest thing with her hair, it did not go unnoticed. Holland was always beautiful to me, but seeing her vulnerability made her even more so.

I waited for her at the front of my car and watched as she made her way toward me. It was still daylight outside, and every part of her flowed with such graceful poise that I was stunned into silence.

"Why are you looking at me like that?" she asked.

"Because you're beautiful," I told her.

Holland stepped into my space and wrapped her arms around my neck. Having her in my arms had quickly become something I never knew I needed. As I looked down into her eyes, a sense of dread filled me. It was the same feeling I got with every passing day, that I tried so hard to ignore.

"Are you okay?" she asked.

I cupped her face in my hand while the other held her close to me and I kissed her. She held tightly to the sleeves of my shirt, and when I deepened the kiss she responded, nipping playfully at my lips.

"I love you," she whispered when we parted.

"You'll love me even more after tonight."

"Oh yeah?"

I kissed the tip of her nose and took her hand in mine, leading her to the door. She looked at the sign overhead and her smile grew.

"Fancy Feet?" she asked. "Are we going dancing?"

"We are," I said.

She jumped into my arms and wrapped her arms around my neck, squeezing tightly.

"I've always wanted to do this! How did you know?"

"I'm just that good," I said.

What I kept to myself was that I had messaged Meg through social media to see if she could help me. After the disaster of the simulator, I needed something that would catch Holland's attention and let her know how much she meant to me. If any of my friends knew I was doing a dance class, they could have skewered me in a second—another reason I chose to do the class in another town.

An older woman walked over and greeted us.

"Are you here for the six o'clock?"

"Yes," I told her.

"Milo?" the woman asked, and I nodded. She then turned her attention to my eager girlfriend. "So that must make you Holland."

"Yes," Holland said.

"Come inside. I'm Madame Georgina and I will be working with you two tonight."

"Is this a private lesson?" Holland whispered as we followed Madame Georgina.

"No," I muttered.

"Please come in and sit on the bench with the others," the teacher instructed. "We're just waiting on one more couple."

Holland and I sat down and looked at the others in the room—our classmates. We were easily the youngest people there, but she did not seem to mind that one bit. She started greeting the others, asking about their dance partners and how long they had been taking lessons. Most of the people there were older than my dad, and for a brief second I thought about how much my mom would have liked to go dancing.

"Okay, everyone, come to the dance floor with your partner and we'll get started."

Holland and I joined the other couples and waited for Madame Georgina to give us instructions. I could feel the people staring at us, so I just kept my eyes on Holland while she told me about her grandparents dancing when she was a kid.

"I used to watch them on Saturday nights when I was little," she said. "They always had so much fun. And Grams would wear these flowy dresses that looked so elegant. She looked like one of those ladies in the old movies she used to watch. Did your parents or grandparents ever do anything like this?"

I shook my head and smiled. "The closest Dad ever got to this were the times that he would walk into the kitchen and pull Mom into his arms so they could dance to whatever song was playing."

"Somehow I can totally see your dad doing that," she said with a smile.

"Mom would try to get away at first, but then he'd say something to her and she would laugh as they started dancing."

It had been a long time since I had allowed myself to think of that time with Mom. There were a few times that I would be sitting and watching them, feeling both awkward and amused by my parents. Mom would always walk over and reach out for my hand. Of course I always resisted because I was embarrassed, but then Dad would give me a look and encourage me to dance. Looking back on those times, I was grateful that I took Mom up on her offer.

"Where'd you go?" Holland asked, squeezing my hand gently.

"I'm right here," I said.

"All right, everyone, we're going to start with some basic steps, so face your partner," Madame Georgina said.

Holland and I stood in front of each other and she started making faces at me, which made me chuckle. I reached out and tickled her side, making her squirm, which caused a few heads to turn in our direction.

"Pay attention," I muttered to her.

She looked at me with mock horror before narrowing her eyes, and I knew she would get me back for trying to embarrass her. The men were instructed to place our right hands on the smalls of the women's backs and hold firmly. Dancing was not something I had ever wanted to do, but seeing how happy Holland was, not to mention having her in my arms, I was more than happy to do that for her.

"Best date ever," Holland said quietly.

"We haven't even started yet," I reminded her.

When she looked up at me, I knew that she was exactly where she wanted to be. I had done that. I had made her smile, and I wanted to make sure that I could make her that happy every day until she left for college. It was not very often that I allowed myself to think of how it would be when she was gone, but in that moment it was all I could think about.

We rarely talked about if we would try to do the long-distance thing because we both knew it would be hard, if not impossible. I was trying to be in the moment, but with the deadline looming over our heads, with each date the ticking clock grew louder.

Madame Georgina interrupted the mood-souring thoughts I was having, and I was grateful. I would think about our impending fate later, but I needed to focus on Holland and making her smile again. The instructor was showing us some foot movements that I could not seem to get.

"I think you have two left feet," Holland whispered teasingly.

"Two left? Are you kidding me?" I laughed.

Before she could stop me, I started moving to the music in the only way I knew how. I had seen those dance shows with my mom when I was younger, and when Dad wasn't around, she would make me practice with her. Dad never knew that Mom was teaching me to dance, but looking back I think she knew she was already sick, and that was her way of teaching me before she was gone.

Picking up new steps was not an easy task for me, but using the moves I knew—piece of cake. I was spinning Holland around and moving around the parquet dancefloor with ease. The other students stood and watched as Holland followed each of my movements with ease while Madame Georgina requested we rejoin the others.

"Come back here," she said. "That's not what I told you to do."

"It's all I know to do," I called out as I danced.

"But I'm trying to teach you," she pleaded.

Holland was laughing as she tried to keep up, and she patted my shoulder. "I take it back. You can dance."

The other couples saw how much fun we were having and started dancing in their own way—some good, some not so good, but all of them were laughing and having fun. Together. The instructor threw up her arms in defeat and watched as her class went rogue. I felt bad because I was not trying to be disrespectful, but seeing how Holland's face light up when I started leading her around the floor was my plan for the night.

"What else don't I know about you?" Holland asked.

"I guess you'll have to stick around to find out," I said with a shrug.

That night, as I drove her home, Holland was quieter than usual. I knew she had enjoyed the dancing, but something must have happened to cause her mood to change. When something bothers me, I need time to process and get my head on straight, so I was trying to give her the same courtesy, but it was hard. All I wanted to do was make her smile and laugh again.

"Are you okay?" I asked.

She looked over at me and smiled. "I'm fine. Just thinking."

"About anything in particular?"

"You."

"Me? And that makes you sad?"

"No. You make me so happy," she said quickly. "It's knowing that I have to leave soon and how much I'm going to miss you."

CHAPTER 21

HOLLAND

Seeing Milo was usually the highlight of my day, but my mind was heavy with a secret I had been keeping to myself for a while. For two months we had spent all of our free time together, and I was risking what we had left by keeping it from him. In my mind it was not that big of a deal, but I knew that logic was wrong. Mom always told me that if I couldn't share a secret with those I loved, then it must not be a good thing.

When I got to his house, I was happy to see that he had not made it home yet: it would have given me a little time to work up the nerve to share what I had found. But then I saw the front door open. Mr. Davis stood in the threshold and waved me in. Reluctantly, I stepped out of my car and walked up the steps where he was waiting for me.

"How ya doin', darlin'?" he asked as I neared the door.

"I'm good. How about you?"

"Can't complain. Milo's running late," Mr. Davis said as he let me into the house.

"Yeah, that's what he said."

"Well there's no need for you to wait outside. Can I get you something to drink?"

"No thanks," I said with a smile.

"Are you okay? You seem a little distracted."

"I'm fine."

"Are you sure?"

I stopped walking and Mr. Davis turned around and cocked his head to the side as he studied me.

"No. I'm not," I admitted nervously. "Do you have a sec?"

"I've got all the time you need. What can I help you with?"

"It's about Milo. Do you think we talk before he gets here?"

"Sure," he said.

We walked into the kitchen and he sat down, so I pulled out a chair across from him. He patiently waited while I gathered up the nerve to say what I had been debating for nearly a week. I loved Milo, and he was my boyfriend, but there was a very real chance that I was treading where I should stay away.

"It's about college."

"I figured as much. Milo said that you leave in August."

"Yes, sir. But this isn't about me…it's about him."

"I know. He's going to be sad to see you go."

I smiled and sighed. I was about to talk to his dad about something I had not discussed with Milo, but if anyone knew him best, it was his dad.

"I'm going to miss him so much. But I did something."

"Okay…I'm listening," he said as he leaned forward and rested his arms on the table.

I took a deep breath and forced myself to speak. "He mentioned before that college wasn't an option. I didn't ask what that meant, but based on other conversations that I've had with him, he really wants to go."

"I saw the acceptance letter," his dad said. "He didn't talk about it much."

"When I've brought it up, he shuts down."

"Same here."

"I really hope I'm not overstepping…but I did some research and I know he's missed the deadlines for the fall, but he could go in the spring. There are all sorts of scholarships and grants that he could apply for."

"But he rejected their acceptance."

"I know. But he could reapply…maybe get in for the spring

179

semester?"

"But you don't want to talk to him about this?"

"I don't know where to start. When we first talked about it, he sort of shut me down almost instantly. And I've never been brave enough to bring it up since."

"So what did you find?"

I reached into my bag and pulled out the folded papers that I had had stashed away for the past week. I had them with me just in case the opportunity ever opened to talk with Milo about it. Somehow the time never seemed right. I had turned into a coward when it came to speaking up, and knew that Mr. Davis would likely have a better chance at pushing the issue.

"I haven't said anything to him," I said. "There's a scholarship available at Westview and Stonewall for children who have lost a parent."

Mr. Davis' eyes widened he nodded. It was hard to tell if I had offended him or if he found that bit of information useful. When Milo and I had talked about college, I had been able to deduce that the family would likely have a hard time paying for it because of the medical bills from when his mom had died. Late one night, I did quite a bit of research and found several scholarships and grants that were available.

Mr. Davis' eyes were sad when he looked at me, but he managed a small nod as he took hold of the papers.

"The other is for engineering majors in the top ten percent of their class who have certain financial needs."

His father was glancing over the papers, and I found myself regretting the decision to broach the conversation with him. I was always aware of those around me before I spoke and tried to not offend anyone, but right then I felt a huge weight on my shoulders.

"I'm so sorry. I shouldn't have said anything."

"No. No, Holland," he said, reaching his hand across the table. He patted the top of my hand and smiled again. "Thank you for caring enough about him to look into this. But I'll take it from here."

"Are you sure?"

"He's my son. I'm sure."

Milo walked in and saw the moment I was sharing with his dad with a strange look on his face. Mr. Davis smiled up at him, and it must have been enough to pacify him because he walked in and patted his dad's shoulder before kissing me hello.

"What are you two talking about?" he asked.

"Holland was just telling me about..."

"Ben and Harper's wedding," I said quickly. "They told us last night that they're going to be moving after the wedding in the fall, and I'm really sad."

At least that was not a total lie. Ben had told me earlier that day about a job offer he had received from one of the engineering firms he had interned with back in the spring. It was a great opportunity, but it still made me sad. Our family was changing and growing up, and I knew things would ultimately be different.

Milo cocked his head to the side and looked at me for a moment before speaking. "But you won't even be around either."

"I know, but I'm not ready for it. I love Harper, she's great...but it'll be weird not seeing him when I come home."

"I'm sorry," Milo said. "I know that'll be hard for you."

I felt like a jerk for lying about why I was talking to his dad, but given how dismissive he was when I tried to talk about him and college, it was my only choice. Maybe not my only choice, because I could have butted out altogether.

Mr. Davis stood up from the table and excused himself. Milo went to sit down and picked up something from the floor.

"Hey Dad," he said as he started to open it up. "You dropped something."

His father had just rounded the corner but returned quickly, reaching for the papers in Milo's hand. But it was too late: he was already reading the scholarship title at the top of the page. Everything slowed as I watched his eyes fill with betrayal—or maybe it was humiliation. It was almost impossible for me to stop what was happening in front of me.

"What's this?" he asked, looking up at his dad.

"It was just something I was looking into—for you," Mr. Davis said.

"I told you that I'm not going," Milo shot back angrily.

"Maybe not right now, but you can."

"Can we not do this right now?"

My eyes were glued to the table in front of me because I was too afraid to look up at either of them. I knew that I had created the mess, and yet I sat like a coward and let his dad take the fall. I should have stepped up right then, but selfishly, I was glad that I wasn't on the receiving end of his ire.

Milo pushed back his seat from the table and stormed out the back door without a word. I looked up at Mr. Davis, who put a consoling hand on my shoulder before walking away in the opposite direction of his son. And there I was, sitting alone in the kitchen, the fallout from my meddling only beginning. It was clear that there was never going to be a right time to have that conversation with Milo, and it was hard for me to understand why.

He was outside for half an hour before I walked out to check on him. My stomach felt like it was twisted in knots and I felt like I needed to leave, but there was no way I was going anywhere before I had gotten a chance to talk to him again. When I finally pushed myself to walk outside, I found Milo sitting on the deck, looking out toward the back fence with a defeated look on his face.

"Hey," I said timidly. "You okay?"

"I'm sorry we did that in front of you."

"It's fine…Maybe we should talk," I said.

Guilt was eating away at me, because for the past two weeks I had researched and found things for Milo and never once mentioned I was doing anything. He even walked in once while I was reading up on a scholarship for which he was qualified. All of this, even with the best of intentions, I was doing behind his back.

"Holland," he said, still not looking at me. "Not now."

"I'm sorry," I said.

He finally looked over at me, his brow furrowed. "Why are you sorry? You didn't do anything wrong."

"But—I did."

"You did what?" he asked.

"It was me."

"What are you talking about?" he asked.

I remained quiet and waited for my words to hit him. When his eyes widened with the realization of what I was saying, it almost immediately shifted the way he looked at me. Milo stayed quiet, and the way he stared at me reminded me of the Milo I had known in school—the one I wanted to know, who seemed to dislike me so much. He told me before that I had been wrong in how I thought he saw me, but in that moment I was certain. He was hurt and disappointed.

"What do you mean?" he asked, his words steady and quiet, like he was hoping he had heard me wrong.

"I was the one who did the research. Your dad was just covering for me."

"Holland," he sighed, looking up at the dimming night sky. "Why would you do that?"

"I'm sorry. I was only trying to help."

"But, if you recall, I didn't ask for help."

"I know…It's just that I know how much you want to go to school."

"It's none of your business," he snapped. "I can't believe you would do that."

"I—"

"No. You know nothing about what I want. No one does. And you're making assumptions that are none of your concern."

"I didn't mean to upset you."

"Upset," he scoffed, repeating my words.

"Milo…"

"I think you should go."

"What? Are you serious?"

I took a step toward him, thinking that it was a joke. There was no way he was that mad over some harmless research, right? His reaction seemed over the top to me, and he refused to explain why.

"Yes. You need to leave."

"Can't we just talk?"

Milo turned his face up to where I stood and looked at me without a hint of emotion. I preferred the anger, annoyance, or hurt in his face to the impassive vibe he was giving me. At least when he showed his feelings, I knew he cared. That was the look of emptiness and the thought of being nothing to him had me scrambling to find some way to make it right.

"That's what you should have done before you went behind my back."

"But you never wanted to talk about it."

"So, to you, that means going behind my back?" His tone was full of accusation.

"I'm sorry. Please, just hear me out."

"I have nothing to say."

He stood up from the table and walked inside the house without another word. When I had started researching, I knew there was a chance that Milo might not be happy with the results I found, but I thought he would at least let me tell him what I learned. But he was far too angry to hear me out.

Hurt and rejected, I walked through the house to leave, hoping that he would try to stop me, but he was gone. Mr. Davis was standing in the living room and he looked toward Milo's room and then at me. He closed his eyes and shook his head before making eye contact with me again.

I'm sorry, he mouthed.

I closed my eyes and nodded once before grabbing my purse and walking out the door. If Milo wanted me to know how insignificant I was to him, it was perfectly clear. I got the hint, and it hurt like hell, but I refused to let him see me break.

CHAPTER 22

MILO

I heard the front door close behind Holland as she left. A part of me wanted to run after her and stop her from leaving, but the other part of me felt like the biggest loser who didn't deserve her. Holland Monroe was the girl of my dreams, the one I had wanted for so long. And when it finally happened—when I won the girl—it sucked to realize that I wasn't enough. She wanted more from me than I was able to give.

As she drove away, I walked into the living room where Dad was watching the local news and scrolling through his phone. He was as guilty as Holland, though I was not clear on his part in the scheme.

"What in the hell was that all about?" I asked.

"Wanna change that tone?" he countered.

"You knew she did that?"

"I found out a few minutes before you," Dad said. "And if you ask me, you were a little too hard on her. She was just trying to help."

"I don't need her help. I'm not a charity case."

"No one said that you are."

"I've gotta get out of here."

I grabbed my keys off the table, but my dad got up from his spot on the couch and quickly snatched them from my hand.

"I need my keys," I snapped, holding my hand open as I waited for him to hand them back.

With a smug smile on his face, he shoved them into his pocket and crossed his arms. There were few times that he put his foot down, and when he did there was no changing his mind.

"Not when you're all pissed off like this. You calm down and you can have your keys back."

"I'm fine," I said, though we both knew it was a lie.

"Great. Then let's talk."

"I'm going to my room," I said as I started to walk away.

There was little he could say that would justify anything that had taken place in the last hour.

"Your mom would be livid if she saw how you just treated your girlfriend."

And he said the exact right words that stopped me in my tracks. As I slowly turned around to face him, Dad's face was both sad and angry. He rarely brought her up to make a point, and I was ready to scream and yell at him for choosing that moment. But as I opened my mouth to argue, he started talking.

"We raised you better than that. Why do you assume that Holland thinks you're a charity case? That girl cares an awful damn lot about you. Do you know that?"

"Yeah," I scoffed. "So much that apparently if I don't go to college, I'm not good enough."

"That's not what she said. In fact, thanks to her I know a little more about my son—since he doesn't care to share anything with his old man."

"Like what?"

"Like the fact that you do really want to go to college. You lied to me, son."

"About what?"

"When I found that admissions letter, you said that you just" wanted to see if you could get in. I knew better, but for some reason I took you at your word."

"I did."

"Yeah, but Holland was telling me that you do really want to go."

"Let's just drop it," I said quickly.

"No. I let you walk away from this discussion before. Now we're going to have it out."

"Have what out?"

"Why didn't you tell me you wanted to go?"

"I don't."

"Damn it, Milo! You're lying."

"What do you want me to say, Dad? That I want to go? You want me to tell you that when that letter came in I was beyond happy that I was accepted? And then when I saw the tuition fees I knew it was never going to happen?"

"I told you…"

"We can't afford it," I snapped, and then took a deep breath to calm myself before I said anything else. "And that's fine. I'll be fine."

"Why didn't you come to me? This is what I'm here for," he said sadly.

"You have enough on your plate without tuition."

"But what about these scholarships?" he asked.

I shook my head and walked over to sit on the couch. I rested my elbows on my knees and stared at the coffee table in front of me. There were few times in my life where I had seen my dad looking so helpless. The first was when Mom was dying; the second—her funeral. I hoped that I would never again see him look like that, but there he was, unable to do anything, and I knew it killed him. That was the reason I had never said anything about the applications or the fact that I had turned all of them down.

"I tried. I didn't qualify. I mean, I got a couple of small ones…They'll help with junior college, but they wouldn't make a dent in the Westview tuition."

"We could get financial aid—kids do it all the time."

"Dad, I don't want to go to college and graduate with hundreds of thousands in debt before I even get a job."

"But Mi…"

"Let it go, Dad. I already did."

"What about the ones that Holland found? Maybe you could get one of them," he said as he opened the piece of paper she gave him. "I mean, from what I can tell, you meet the requirements. Four-point GPA, National Honor Society, top ten percent, deceased parent…"

"What?" I asked, reaching for the paper that he was reading.

My eyes scanned the paper, reaching the bullet points that Dad had named. I had never seen those particular scholarships, but then again I had never thought of exploiting my mother's death to get college benefits. I crumpled the paper up and tossed it onto the table.

"If I ever do go to college, it won't be because I'm using Mom's death," I snapped as I stood up to leave the room.

"Sit down," Dad ordered.

I knew that tone well, and it was not one to be messed with, so I sat and waited for the lecture. For the most part, Dad and I had a system between us that worked: I studied, got good grades, worked, and helped pay the bills. Dad did everything else. We rarely argued, and he let me do what I needed to do without interfering much. When he did have something to stay, he would stand his ground until his point was made.

"What did your mom want for you?"

"What are you talking about?"

"What's the one thing that she always told you."

"All she ever said was that she wanted me to be happy."

"Exactly. And if college makes you happy, that's what she would want for you. And being eligible because she died doesn't mean that you're exploiting her. It doesn't mean that you miss her any less. Other kids go through the same thing, and if someone set up a scholarship to help kids like you, why not?"

"That's not how I'm going to get there."

"It's not an insult to your mother if you do."

"I'm done talking about this."

Dad was not about to give me my keys, so I walked back into my room and lay down, staring up at the ceiling. If other people wanted the scholarship money, they could have it. When I tried to think of the things Mom had said to me while she was still alive, I would try to hear her voice. The older I got, the less I heard her voice and the more I heard my own. Maybe Dad was right and she would want me to at least pursue it, but what I wanted had not even been a consideration when Holland had decided to look into options for me.

My phone buzzed inside my pocket and I knew it was her before I even looked at the screen. I never thought I could be as angry with her as I was that day.

Holland: Can we please talk?

I read her words and set the phone down beside me. There was nothing I wanted to hear from her, and I knew if I did speak there was a strong chance I would say something I would regret.

Holland: I know you're mad at me. I'm sorry.

I stared at the screen—at her apology—and my anger grew. Was I stupid to consider that I was enough just as I was? I had known when we started dating that it would end when she left for college, and I had gone for it anyway. And I fell in love with the girl who I had liked for years. It was my own fault for believing that we were special, that maybe we could be the couple that overcame distance. Hell, we couldn't even overcome secrets— because she kept them.

Me: Ok

It was the only thing I could respond. She knew I had read her messages, but there was nothing I wanted to say. She needed to give me time to process and get over it, but it was not in Holland's nature to let things go. If she could get ahead of it, she could fix the problem. And that was when I realized that she saw me as something she needed to fix. But I was not broken.

Holland: Can we talk after work?

Perhaps I was an asshole, because instead of answering, I left her on read.

I knew if I stayed there in my room I was going to get angrier with Holland. I needed to get out, so I called Ethan and asked him to come pick me up. He always had something going on, and I knew that a distraction was exactly what I needed. He was at my house within thirty minutes, and Dad barely said a word to me as I walked out the door.

"Where are we going?" I asked Ethan when I climbed inside his car.

"Knox is having another party. Want to head there?"

"Yeah. Whatever."

"Should we get Holland?"

"She's busy," I lied.

Ethan looked over at me and seemed like he was about to question my lie, but instead pulled out of the driveway and drove us to Knox's. The last time I was at his house I had missed my opportunity to talk to Holland, but lucky for me it had all worked out. She had been the best part of my summer, but then it had all gone to hell. I knew I was being slightly over the top in my reaction, but there were things I could not quite understand—one of those being why she had never asked me in the first place.

"You sure you don't want to call her?" Ethan asked as we reached Knox's house.

"Yeah."

Satisfied with my answer, he turned the engine off and we walked up to the front door to find ourselves greeted by none other than our friend Hunter. He was already on his way to being completely wasted, and I envied his current state. I had never been much of a drinker, but I needed something to help me out of my piss-poor mood.

"Damn!" Hunter said as he craned his neck to look around me. "Where's your better half?"

I noticed Ethan shake his head and gesture for Hunter to back off, but even sober, that was not something he would ever do.

"She wise up and dump your ass?" Hunter laughed.

My body tensed and I felt Ethan clap his hand against my back, pushing me through the door. There were probably fifty or so people spread throughout the house that I could see. And still, I found myself looking around for Holland. As much as I needed to avoid her, I wanted her.

I said my hellos to the people I knew as I walked into the kitchen and grabbed a beer from the cooler. Hunter looked at me and then to Ethan before taking a swig of his beer. As many times as I had been the designated driver for them, it was their turn—and I proved that by downing one beer and immediately grabbing another.

"All right…so it's that kind of night," Hunter said.

Ethan stood next to me and nodded without saying a word. He had my back, and that was all I needed to know before making the entire shitty day disappear from memory. If even only for a short time.

CHAPTER 23

HOLLAND

It was dark when I finally pulled into my driveway. I typed several texts to Milo, hoping that maybe he would respond, and he did. Until my last message. I stared at it and waited for his response, but there was nothing. He left me on read, and I wanted to strangle him because he knew I found that so annoying.

Mom and Dad were watching a movie in the living room when I got home. I tossed my purse onto the floor and sat down, still shocked from Milo's reaction. When they saw how upset I was, they paused the movie and looked at me but I remained quiet.

"You're home early," Mom said.

"I know," I sighed sadly before looking at her.

Mom's eyes looked sad, and I loved that she understood me without a word having to be spoken. Every time I replayed what had happened, I felt a mixture of remorse and anger.

"Okay. But why?" Dad asked, looking between Mom and me.

Now Dad was different. He never wanted to wait for me to come around, and rarely caught my nonverbal cues. I had to paint him a picture, and while I was not ready to talk about it, I was the one who had walked in pouting, and I didn't want them to worry.

"Milo's mad at me."

"What? Why?" he asked.

"I don't want to talk about it."

"Okay," Mom said, but Dad would not let it stop there.

"Sometimes talking it out loud helps," Dad said as Mom shook her head slightly.

"I'm not sure that's the case here. Talking is what got me into this mess."

"Okay. Now I need details," Mom said.

I took a deep breath and felt myself angry at Milo's reaction. I was only trying to help, but that was not something he wanted to hear. Maybe he needed more time to process what he perceived as an insult. It was obvious by his reaction that I overstepped, but he was acting as if I had stood on the side of the road with a sign trying to collect money for him. All I did was research.

"We can't help if you don't talk to us," Mom coaxed.

I started to tell them all about what I had done, starting with how it was that I had come to search for the scholarships in the first place. Both remained quiet while I talked the whole thing out, and seemed to understand where I was coming from—which was why I was shocked by their reactions.

"Honey, you had the best of intentions, but you were out of line," Dad said.

"But I was trying to help."

"Hollz," Mom said, placing her hand on mine, "he didn't ask for help. And it was pretty presumptuous of you to assume that it was okay to do this."

"Are you serious?"

I stood up and looked at my parents, who were supposed to be on my side. Was I so wrong? If Marcie were home, I knew she would have sided with me. There was no malice in what I had done; it was strictly informational. What Milo decided to do—or not—with the information, was for him to decide.

"Imagine how it looks to him. His girlfriend is leaving for school and that's going to be hard enough for the both of you. But now, it's like you're telling him he's not good enough for you as he is—college or not," Dad said.

"I don't care if he decides that he doesn't want to go to college," I argued. "It was never about him having to go anywhere. But he told me that he wants to go. I just wanted to make sure he had all the information before he made a decision one way or the other. Milo is the most amazing guy I've ever been with. I love him…I wasn't trying to hurt him."

"Then why didn't you talk to him about it before you started? Clearly there was a part of you that knew he didn't want this. Otherwise it wouldn't have been a secret," Mom said.

Her words echoed in my ears and I knew she was right. I hated to admit it, but she was. I had struggled with my decision to share the information, and instead I had dragged his dad into it. As I replayed the evening in my head, I saw things from Milo's point of view and my heart broke. If he, for one second, thought that I wanted him any less because he was staying home, he was mistaken. He was the only reason I hated the idea of leaving—the thought of being without him hurt more than I could tell him.

"Thanks for listening," I said as I said goodnight.

Milo and I were supposed to go to a drive-in movie, one of our date night bucket list things, but all of that was tossed when he had asked me to leave. A combination of hurt and indignation started to flood my veins. Milo was clearly not taking my calls, but that didn't mean I had to sit at home and feel sorry for myself. Usually Meg would be my first call, but she was too far away to do anything so I called Colin and asked him to pick me up.

***

"Where are we going?" he asked when I got into his car.

"I don't care. Wherever you want. I just can't sit around the house."

"Where's Milo?"

I looked over at Colin and raised a brow, as if that was answer enough. He scoffed playfully and nodded his head. I liked that we could communicate so easily without uttering a word. When he squeezed my hand, I knew he would take care of me, and that was all I needed to know.

As we pulled up to Knox's place, I was not the least bit surprised that Colin had chosen the one place we both knew would have something going on. His parties were frequent and always fun—exactly what I needed. We walked to the house, passing a sea of cars along the way.

"I got ya tonight," Colin said, and I knew that I was safe.

I gave him a hug and we walked inside, hand in hand. We were greeted by several familiar faces, and loud voices trying to drown out the music. I felt myself relax, because for the first time since I had left Milo's house, I couldn't hear myself think—and that was exactly what I needed. As I headed toward the kitchen, I spotted Ethan, who was waving at us.

"Hey, Hollz," he said, kissing my cheek. "How's it goin'?"

"Could be better," I said.

Ethan turned around, grabbed a shot glass, and handed it to me. When I looked at Colin, he nodded his head, and again I knew I was okay because he had my back. I quickly downed the shot before thinking better of it, and winced when the awful-tasting liquor slid down my throat. I had never been much of a drinker, and perhaps the stupidest time to drink was out of anger.

"That should help," Ethan laughed. "Here, have one more. You need it."

I didn't *need* it. But I took it anyway and swallowed it without a second thought. Colin took the glass from me and set it down on the counter.

"That's good for now," he said.

"Yeah, I agree," Ethan said. "That should make it easier."

"Make what easier?" I asked.

He pointed toward the living room and I looked over his shoulder to see my boyfriend sitting with a bunch of people laughing and carrying on like nothing had ever happened that day. Colin placed his hand on my shoulder and I took a deep breath. There was no way I was going into that room, because not only did I not want to make a scene, but it was obvious that he was in a good mood. That was exactly how I wanted to feel, too, so I

195

reached into the fridge and grabbed a beer, walking in the opposite direction of where Milo was sitting.

The two of us had spent so much time together that neither of us had done much with our friends unless we were together. I would give him that space, and I would take it for myself as well. There was a massive sunroom off to the right of the front door, so I walked in and found several of my classmates hanging out.

"Holland!" Melanie shouted when she spotted me.

My grin spread and I ran over to the couch where she was sitting and dropped myself into the free spot next to her and Colin followed. I had known Mel since we were kids, and though we had drifted apart, she was someone that had always been the kindest and most genuine person. She and Hunter had started dating around the same time that Milo and I did, but from the looks of it, they were doing pretty good.

"Hey, she's mine," Hunter laughed, wrapping his arm around Mel. "Do you know how long it took me to get her to finally agree to date me? You can't just swoop in and take her away."

"I've known her longer. I win," I said, playfully tugging her toward me.

When I let go, she settled into Hunter's embrace and smiled at me. Though I looked happy on the outside, inside I was envious of them. They were together, happy, enjoying the time they had left until summer ended. They would be going to college in different states, but they didn't let that stop them.

We chatted for a while about the summer and catching up on the latest gossip. I took a sip of the beer I had grabbed, but when I took a swig I realized quickly that I was not a beer fan. Hunter readily took the beverage from me, drinking it himself. It didn't matter to me because I was already feeling the effects of the shots I had taken in the kitchen.

"Where's Milo?" Hunter asked.

I had been with them for nearly thirty minutes, and it was the first time anyone had asked me about him. Milo was at the party, but we were not there together. It was a question I was not prepared to answer. But before I could speak, I heard his voice answer from across the room. Butterflies swarmed in my stomach and I looked over to see him standing in the doorway.

"Are you drunk?" Hunter laughed.

Milo shrugged his shoulders and then looked at me. It was hard to tell if he was still angry with me, because the way he was staring at me sent tingles up my arms. Maybe it was the liquor I had imbibed, or maybe it was just Milo. All I knew was that I had never seen him look at me with such intensity.

"Got a sec?" he asked, still looking at me.

"Not right now," I said. "Colin and I were about to leave."

"Please?"

I gently elbowed Colin's side and he nodded as he helped me to my feet. We walked together to where Milo stood, and the two exchanged tense greetings. My friend was not aware of the details of why Milo and I were fighting, but he was on my side. That was why he was also one of my best friends.

"I'll be right back," Colin said, more for Milo's benefit than mine.

He walked toward the kitchen, leaving Milo and me standing in the hallway alone. He was wearing a gray T-shirt with his cargo shorts, his hair hidden beneath a baseball cap.

"Now you want to talk?" I asked.

He shook his head, and before I realized what was happening, he wrapped his arms around my waist and pulled me into a kiss. This was not like the tender and sweet kisses I was used to from Milo. It was urgent and messy, but I didn't bother to resist. My arms snaked around his neck, holding him as close as I could while he deepened the kiss, his tongue plunging into my mouth.

Somewhere nearby, we heard someone clear their throat and it put an end to the impromptu make-out session. Both of us were breathless when we parted, and he moved away, staring at my lips. As he took a step to walk away, I reached out for his hand to stop him and he stared where we were joined. It was then that I realized that he still had not truly looked at me. I moved so he was forced to look into my eyes, and when he did, I said the only thing that came to mind.

197

"I love you."

Before he could answer, or worse, not—I released his hand stepped back, making my way to Colin, who was waiting for me at the front door. When we walked outside, I started to laugh sardonically.

"Do you think a drunken make-out counts as a bucket list date?"

Colin looked at me, his brows pinched, and I nodded.

"Yes. Most definitely," I answered for myself.

I grabbed my phone out of my pocket and started to text Milo, but Colin snatched it from my hand before I could do anything. As I tried to reach for it, he tucked my phone into his pocket and wrapped an arm over my shoulder.

"Let's wait until tomorrow to do that."

"Why?"

"You know why," he said.

"Because you're no fun?"

"Because whatever it was that happened between you two today was not fixed with a drunken kiss. So deal with it when you have a clear head tomorrow. Okay?"

I wanted to argue, but his logic confused me. Colin grinned and kissed the top of my head, and we started walking toward his car.

"What if he wants to break up?" I asked aloud the question I did not even want to have in my head.

Colin stopped moving and stepped in front me, bending down so that we were eye to eye. "Then he doesn't deserve you."

As one of my best friends, he was obligated to say such things, but I knew the truth. I had screwed up, and if I wanted things to work out, I would have to make amends. Somehow.

CHAPTER 24

HOLLAND

"Milo?"

"I'm busy," he said without even looking at me.

"But…"

"This isn't the time or the place," he said dismissively.

Carlo looked at me and shrugged before returning his attention to the dish he was preparing. Rejected once again, I straightened my shoulders back and went to check on my table.

It was another busy night in the restaurant, and after my talk with Hendricks there were only a few more of those on the schedule. She had hired a new waiter, who was already training. He would soon be taking over my shifts, because she needed someone who would be able to work after I left town.

After handing my customers their check, I processed their credit card and cleaned the table after they left. When I walked back to drop the items off in the kitchen, I chanced a look at Milo, who did not make an effort to spare a glance in my direction. I sighed and walked over to Daphne to let her know I was taking my break.

"Trouble with the boyfriend?" Brandon asked in a snarky tone as I walked past him.

As much as I tried to avoid him, he was always around in some capacity. I had learned to either ignore him or say something snappy in return, but I was out of energy that night. Dejected and sad, I looked up at him and sighed before walking outside to get some air.

For three days, Milo had given me the cold shoulder. I had apologized and tried to give him space, but then he had kissed me, confusing the hell out of me.

The next day, I had figured that I needed to make the first move and call him, but he had avoided my calls. I had turned to texting and he had continued to leave me on read. If he wanted to hurt me, he was doing a pretty great job, and I was starting to feel like the girl who refused to get a clue.

"You okay?" I heard Brandon's voice ask from behind me.

His tone lacked the contempt and ire he had leveled against me since I had rejected him in June, but I was still wary. If nothing else, I had learned that Brandon was one of those guys who was only interested in two things: sex and getting his own way.

"I'm fine," I muttered.

"You don't look fine."

"What the hell do you care?"

"I don't. I'm just taking my break."

He lit his cigarette and walked to one of the tables that were on the far side of the area.

I was thankful he was leaving me alone with my own thoughts, but I should have known he wasn't going to stay quiet.

"This was bound to happen," he said loudly from where he was perched on the table.

"Excuse me?" I asked, turning to face him.

"Everyone knows you two broke up."

"We didn't break up," I argued.

Brandon scoffed and exhaled, a plume of smoke dissipating around him. I turned around and looked at my phone, hoping that maybe Milo had seen me go outside. Maybe he would find me and we could talk or something.

"Details," he grumbled. "If it didn't happen, it will. It was always going to end like this."

"You don't know anything about me and Milo or what's going on."

"Oh yeah?" he asked, taking another drag of his cigarette. "You're leaving in what—three weeks? And what's Milo going to do? Stay here and wait for you to come back because you've promised each other that you'll figure it out?"

"Shut up, Brandon," I said, rolling my eyes, but really his words were cutting me deeper than anything I had thought to myself. Milo and I had not allowed ourselves to talk about what happened when the time came for me to leave.

"Everyone always thinks they're special, they're going to be that one percent that actually makes it, but that's not how this works. It was never going to work. You're not special, Holland. No one is. And the sooner you figure that out, the easier it'll be for you to leave."

It felt like someone had sucker punched me. Brandon said, out loud, everything that I had thought but was too scared to say. Maybe it was the end for Milo and me. Maybe we had been fooling ourselves to let it get that far. I had told him in the beginning that I was going to fall for him, and I had. But I had also said I was going to be crushed when it was over.

Was it over?

Was Milo too much of a coward to end it with me? Was he just waiting for me to get the hint?

Tears started streaming down my face and there was nothing I could do to stop them. I wasn't sobbing uncontrollably, like when my dog had passed, but the tears fell just as easily.

"I'm sorry," Brandon said. "I shouldn't have said that."

"Why? Because you suddenly care if you're being a jerk?"

I sank onto the bench behind me and dropped my head into my hands as his words continued to echo in my ears. Brandon left his spot on the table and walked toward me, making sure to give me my space. When I looked up at him, his brows were pinched together in concern, but I shook my head.

"I'm fine."

I'd spent so much time trying to apologize and get Milo to talk to me, and done everything I could to keep myself busy. I had finally hit the wall that took everything out of me. Or rather Brandon had made me hit that wall with his truth bombs.

It took me a couple of minutes to get my emotions under control, while Brandon stood by silently watching. My hurt began to turn to anger that Milo had avoided me. I had tried to make amends, but it was like he was taking it too far. There was no explanation for why he was so mad at me, other than I had overstepped.

I wiped my eyes and took a deep breath before looking at Brandon.

"Can you tell I've been crying?"

He shrugged nonchalantly. "Only because of the puffy eyes and red nose."

I rolled my eyes and scoffed. "Thanks."

"Anytime."

"It wasn't really a *thank you*...You're the reason I look like this."

"No. Milo is."

"Shut up," I said as I started to walk back toward the door.

Once inside, I spotted Daphne, who was talking to Christina. She saw the door open and close behind me, and then she saw Brandon. She cocked her head to the side and raised a concerned brow. I quickly shook my head to tell her I was okay, but she still waved me over anyway.

"Give me a few minutes and then we'll talk," Daphne said before walking to her office.

I stood there and felt like I was counting away the seconds until I could talk to my boss. Quitting was never my go-to for anything; I liked to make things work. But it was time. Between getting ready to leave for Westview, the cut in my shifts, and my relationship with Milo, it was time to walk away. While I loved working at Pine Bridge, one of the things that made me happiest was working alongside my boyfriend—who had effectively iced me out.

I looked over at Milo and sighed as I rounded the corner to talk to Daphne. She was sitting at her desk when I walked in, and asked me to take a seat.

"Are you okay?"

"Yeah, I'm fine. Just a long week."

"Holland, it's only Tuesday."

"I know," I laughed. "Long week."

"You looked like you were crying, and then I see Brandon walk in behind you—so I just need to make sure that everything is okay."

"It's fine."

She raised a brow and I shook my head. "It's not Brandon."

Daphne sighed and nodded her head sadly. "I noticed that you and Milo haven't spoken much. Did you two break up?"

"No…At least I don't think so."

"If you ever need to talk, I'm here."

"I appreciate it. I do. And I do need to talk to you, but not about Milo."

She sat up straighter and folded her arms on her desk as she leaned forward. "Shoot."

"I need to give my notice."

"You…but you don't leave for another three weeks."

"Now that Justin has finished training, I'm not getting as many shifts."

Daphne opened her mouth to speak, but I continued talking.

"And I don't blame you. Truly. I just think I need to leave now and start getting everything together for the move."

"Are you sure? I can give you more shifts."

"No. I think it's time."

"I was just working on the schedule for next week. What do you want me to do?"

"Go ahead and give Justin my shifts. I'll finish out this week, if that's okay with you."

"No, it's not okay, Holland. I hate to see you go. But I

understand," she said, before changing the subject back to him. "What are you going to do about Milo?"

"I don't have any more tables. I'm going to clean up my section and call it a night. If he's still around, maybe I'll get a chance to talk to him."

Daphne placed her arms on the desk as she leaned forward with a smile. "I want to say that I have loved having you work here. We're going to miss you."

"Thank you so much for everything," I said as I stood up.

I walked out of her office and into the main dining area. It took me another thirty minutes before I had everything done and I was ready to leave. I waited until Jaysen walked away before approaching Milo to see if we could talk. He must have sensed my presence because his entire posture changed as I neared, and I hated that he would have that sort of reaction. Three days before, he had needed to be with me as much as possible, but now it felt like he couldn't get far enough away.

"Hey," I said, standing next to him.

"Holl…"

"I'm done trying," I said quietly. "I don't want to be done, but you've given me no choice. I get the hint. But I want you to know something and I really need you to look at me when I say it. Please?"

He took a deep breath and looked over at me, his face impassive. I felt like it was the last time I would see him, and I found myself trying to memorize every detail of his face. I had enough pictures of the two of us together in my phone, but knowing that I wouldn't get to stare into those familiar eyes hurt in ways I had never imagined.

"It was never about whether or not you went to college. That didn't matter to me. I just wanted you to have everything you wanted. I know I overstepped, and I'm sorry. You won't see me anymore because I just gave my notice. I only have two more shifts, and you're off those days. So you won't have to worry about seeing me."

Milo opened his mouth to speak, but I held up my hand to stop him.

"Despite everything, this has been the most amazing summer and I'm glad that I spent it falling in love with you."

I leaned forward and kissed his cheek. Had he turned his face a fraction more toward me, my lips would have been on his, and it seemed that he thought the same. Neither of us moved, and for a moment things felt almost normal between us. But when I heard Jaysen say something, his voice growing closer to where Milo and I stood, I moved away without another word. Milo had heard me out, and that was all had wanted.

When I slipped out the back door, I felt the tears begin to threaten, so I hurried to my car, slamming the door shut behind me. As my heart shattered, the tears spilled down my face. I guess Brandon was right: it had ended the way it was always going to end.

CHAPTER 25

HOLLAND

Things with Milo were actually over. He had barely even acknowledged me at Knox's place—not that I had gone out of my way to talk to him either. He seemed to be avoiding me both in person and via text, and I refused to be that girl...the one who did not seem to get the hint. So my final goodbye two days earlier was still fresh, the wound unable to heal that quickly.

Being with him during the summer had made me happy, but that changed when he started to phase me out. There had to be more to his attitude toward me than just my looking up some scholarships. Maybe I would know what that was if he bothered to speak to me.

When I talked to Meg about the fight, she was able to see both sides of it and placed blame equally on Milo and me. Though she was my best friend and should have been Team Holland all the way, I was glad she didn't choose to tell me what she thought I wanted to hear. But it still didn't make me happy to be second best.

My summer was quickly coming to an end, and though it had started out amazingly, it was ending up being a damn crap-fest:

absent best friend, about to leave my home for good, and a boyfriend that didn't seem to want that title anymore—I was starting to feel worse about my situation every day.

With my job at the country club at an end, the past few days had been spent packing boxes, bingeing Netflix, and spending the evenings with my parents. In fact, I was in the middle of packing up a box to take to Westview with me when I heard a loud knock sound at the door.

"Hollz, can you get that?" Mom yelled from somewhere in the house.

Mom and I had spent much of the day shopping for things I would need in my dorm, and had ended it with an early dinner, just the two of us. I felt bad because I had been spending so much time with Milo that it rarely left enough time to be with Mom and Dad. But I was lucky that they had encouraged me to do things with him because they liked him—though I had kept mum on the recent turn our relationship had taken.

"Yeah," I called out as I walked to the door. "Are you expecting someone?"

When she didn't answer I thought nothing of it, until I opened the door. To my surprise, it was a welcome and familiar face.

"Is there a Holland Monroe here?"

"Meg?" I yelled, jumping into my best friend's arms. "What are you doing here?"

"It's good to see you too," she laughed, returning my hug.

The tears started rolling as I continued to hug her tighter than I ever had before. I had been lost without her, but I had had no idea how lost until that moment. It was like being reunited with my other half, and I knew ours was a friendship that I would treasure.

"Are you crying?" she asked.

I shook my head but did not utter a word because then she would know for sure that I was, in fact, crying.

"Aw," she cooed. "I missed you too."

"I can't believe you're here," I said as I finally released her from my grasp. "Why didn't you tell me?"

"And miss this reaction? Not in a million years."

"There she is," Mom said as she walked in behind me. She greeted Meg with a big hug and then stepped aside so she could come in.

"You knew Meg was coming to town?"

"Of course," Mom said. "Who do you think talked her into visiting?"

"Admittedly, she didn't have to try too hard. I was terribly homesick."

"How long are you in town?"

"A week. So let's get going."

"What?" I looked down at my clothes and then at Meg, who shrugged. "I can't go anywhere looking like this."

"Then you better get changed."

"Where are we going?"

"I called Colin. We're going out."

"He's actually doing something without Chris?"

"I told him it's just the three of us...no boyfriend. Besides, he couldn't argue since he did it already once for you."

"I can't believe he went for that," I laughed. "Okay, I'll be right back. Hopefully I didn't pack everything up already."

***

Colin, Meg, and I being together again was exactly what I needed. Oddly, neither brought up the subject of Milo, which meant Meg and Colin had talked about it between the two of them already. Honestly, I was grateful to not have to answer the questions about what had happened and if we were broken up.

"Where am I going?" I asked Meg as I continued to drive.

"I'll tell you when to turn when it's time," she said before turning her head to face Colin in the back seat. "So how's Chris handling the impending long-distance thing?"

"He's not," Colin said. "We're breaking up."

"What?" Meg and I asked in unison.

"Why?" I added.

"We're eighteen," he answered, as if it was enough, but when neither of us was satisfied with that response, he explained. "It rarely works. I want it to, but I think we're being realistic."

"Why do you sound okay about that?" I asked. "You and Chris have been together for over a year."

"Trust me, there's nothing about me that's okay with this. But what else can I do? This was his idea and I went along for his sake."

"I'm sorry," I said.

"Turn right up here," Meg said.

"Are we going to the drive-in?" I asked excitedly.

"Yep." She beamed proudly.

I felt my eyes sting with unshed tears, because that was something on my list to do with Milo. We had never gotten around to it, but Meg knew all about it and she was doing that just for me.

"Do you know, I've never been here," Colin said.

"Me either," I admitted. "I was going to take…I was gonna go last weekend."

"Milo," Colin said. "You were going to take Milo."

"Yeah," I said as I pulled into the parking lot to pay the attendant.

The guy directed us to park anywhere we wanted, but Meg was very specific that she wanted to watch from the middle, because that was where the view was the best.

"If I knew we were coming here, I would have packed snacks," I said.

"I got that covered," Meg answered.

She reached into the back seat and grabbed her purse. When she opened it, she revealed enough candy to send the three of us into a sugar coma. I was surprised because neither of us had a sweet tooth to that extent, but she had covered her bases.

"I need something to drink," Colin said. "You got anything like that in your bag, *Mary Poppins*?"

Meg laughed and shook her head. "Colin and I will go grab some drinks. What do you want, Hollz?"

"Water is fine with me."

The two of them climbed out of the car and walked to the concession stand. I couldn't help but think of Milo and the rest of the plans that we had had together. He had promised to take me to the skating and I had been so excited that I would finally get to see him on ice skates. But sometimes things don't work out the way we plan.

When the car door opened, I looked over, stunned to see Milo sitting next to me. I looked at him and then outside my window. He glanced at me and then looked at the screen in front of us. His arm was stretched to my seat, and he grinned as if the last five days never happened.

"What are you doing?" I asked.

"I'm watching a movie."

"Milo. What are you doing *here*?"

"We're on a date."

"What are you talking about?"

His smile faded and he turned his body so he was facing me. All traces of humor were gone, and he started to reach out for my hand but stopped, his hand flexing slightly as he placed it on his leg.

"Is this some sort of joke?" I asked.

"I knew that if I called or texted you, there was a strong chance you wouldn't agree to go out with me—not that I blame you."

"You've avoided me for the last five days," I said.

"Look…I have never loved anyone like I love you. But I was mad. I didn't stop loving you."

"Well, nothing says 'I love you' like silence," I snapped.

"You made me hear you out the other day. Now it's your turn to listen to me." He paused. "When I told you that college wasn't feasible right now, that was the truth. I just didn't explain why."

"You don't have to tell me," I told him, my voice quiet. "You were right, it's none of my business."

"But I need to tell you."

"Okay."

"When my mom was sick, the medical bills piled up, and they just kept coming even after she died. I help out and I see the bills—it's pretty bad. I can't add the burden of college onto my dad. And I refuse to go into debt for college."

"I get it," I answered.

"I applied for several scholarships, and I got a few, but I'll be lucky if they buy books," he admitted. "But the big ones, I didn't meet all the criteria. It's been one hit after another. And then when you told me about the ones you found, I was pissed. In my head, you were telling me that I wasn't good enough…"

"That's not it at all."

"But…I also didn't want to use my mom's death as a bullet point that tells me I meet some morbid gauge to get money."

"I'm so sorry," I said, trying to fight off an oncoming wave of tears. "It was never my intention to disrespect your mom. I swear."

Milo finally took my hand in his, and a feeling of calm spread through me. I had missed being with him and holding him in any way I could. He kissed my hand and looked at me.

"I know that. I knew it then too. But I guess somewhere in the back of my head, I was waiting for the other shoe to drop. You're leaving soon, and maybe a part of me was just letting you go. But I heard you the other day," he said. "At work, when you said goodbye I hated it."

"It wasn't great for me either," I admitted. "I got into my car and cried because we broke up."

"But we didn't. I just needed a little more time."

"For what?"

"To make it up to you. I had to prove to Meg and Colin that I wasn't a jerk and that I wanted to make things right with you."

"*You* got Meg to come home?" I asked, and he nodded.

"I needed them to get you here so we could do the date we didn't get to do."

"But I'm leaving in two weeks," I reminded him.

He reached out and tucked a stray hair behind my ear, grazing my cheek along the way. "I'd rather spend the rest of this summer with you, and miss you when you're gone, than lose you and miss out on the best parts."

"Me too."

"Is it okay if I kiss you now?" he asked.

"The movie started," I whispered.

"Screw the movie. You don't go to the drive-in to watch the

movie anyway," he chuckled as he leaned in to kiss me.

"Wait," I said, pulling my face away and looking around. "Where's Meg and Colin?"

"They went out. They were just supposed to get you here to be with me."

"What if I didn't want you here?"

"Look at your texts," he said.

I pulled out my phone and saw that I had a message from Meg.

Meg: *If you want me to leave, just say so.*

I grinned and looked up at Milo. He gave me a lopsided smile and waited for me to decide what I wanted to do.

Me: *Call me tomorrow.*
Meg: *Ok. Have fun.*

As soon as I set the phone down, Milo leaned over to give me the kiss that had been interrupted. We had lost five days, but I would spend the next two weeks making sure we made the most of the time we had left.

CHAPTER 26

MILO

Holland and I spent our last evening together at my house. Dad was supposed to have dinner with us, our final send-off for her before she left for college. At the last minute he got a call to come in for some overtime work, and it was hard for him to turn it down. The three of us ate a quick meal and then he rushed out, hugging Holland before he ran out the door.

"I'm gonna miss your dad," she said.

"He's gonna miss you too," I said.

She nodded her head, and I stood up from the table and began taking the plates to the kitchen. Holland started to pick up her plate but I stopped her.

"You go sit and watch TV or something. I'll clean up and then we can watch a movie."

"I'd rather sit in here with you."

I was halfway through the dishes when I realized that I could take care of all of that later. My time with Holland was running out, so I stopped and leaned against the counter to watch her as she scrolled through her phone.

213

"Why are you looking at me like that?" she asked when she looked up at me.

"I have something to tell you."

"I'm listening."

"Dad and I have been talking, and I'm going to apply for a few of those scholarships that you found."

"Are you really?" she asked, her eyes wide as she smiled.

"Yeah. It took some convincing, but Dad's right: this is what Mom would want."

"I'm so happy for you."

"Well, I wouldn't have done it if it hadn't been for you. We'll see what happens, but if all goes well I might be enrolled in college in the spring."

She stood up and walked over to me, wrapping her arms around my neck. I held her tightly against me, never tiring of having her close to me. It was never long enough or close enough, but I would take whatever I could get.

"Whatever you do, I know it'll be amazing," she said before kissing me.

Holland's phone started buzzing in her hand, so she walked off to answer it. I decided to finish the dishes that were left, which wasn't too many, and then walked off to find her.

"Hollz? Where are you?"

I walked into my bedroom and saw her looking at the pictures on my dresser. She had seen all of them before and asked me about my mom, but this time it like she was memorizing every detail. I was trying to commit to memory every detail about *her*. I walked over and stood behind her, wrapping my arms around her waist.

"You okay?"

"No," she whispered. "I don't want to leave you."

"I know. But you have to go."

"I know," she answered. "What's going to happen to us?"

I turned her around in my arms and she stared up at me, forcing a smile. I kissed her briefly and cupped her face in my hand. It was the one subject we had avoided since our first night together, but it was always looming overhead.

"Whatever you want to happen."

"I love you so much."

"I love you too."

I hated to see her so sad. I didn't want our last night together to be spent with tears or thinking the worst, so I spun her around repeatedly until she was laughing for me to stop. Once I stopped twirling her, I pulled her into my arms and started dancing even though no music was playing.

The sound of her laughter was exactly what I needed, and I kept doing it until we were both breathless from laughing. I held her in my arms and we fell back onto my bed, staring up at the ceiling until we caught our breaths. Holland was lying on my arm and I wrapped my free one over her, pulling her into a hug. She was tucked safely in my arms and I wanted to keep her there as long as possible.

She surprised me when I felt her lips brush against the base of my neck. Everything inside me took notice, but I remained still until she freed her hands that were against my chest and trailed them until they were wrapped around the back of my neck. As Holland pulled me over her, I stared into the eyes of this person that I loved more than I loved anything else. I let her take the lead, but every part of me was ready for whatever she wanted.

"I love you, Milo."

"I love you, too."

Holland tugged at her shirt, pulling it over her head, and tossed it onto the floor. I could have stared at her forever, but there was no time because her hands were reaching for my shirt that was between us. As I shed the clothing that separated us, she pulled me against her, her mouth working against mine as we took the one step we had never even discussed. My arms trembled as I held myself over her, giving her a chance to change her mind, but she closed the space between, leaving no doubt what she wanted.

***

"Let me get that," I said, taking the box from Mrs. Monroe's arms.

She smiled and willingly let the box go. I had spent the morning at their house helping load all of Holland's boxes into the bed of Mr. Monroe's truck. There were still a few boxes left, but Westview was only three hours away and her parents planned to bring them to her in a couple of weeks.

I placed the box in the truck bed and closed the gate. Seeing all of her things packed away was the final reminder that our time had finally come to an end.

"We'll be right back," her mom said to us. "Dad and I are going to get some gas and give you two a few minutes to say your goodbyes."

As they drove off, Holland and I walked inside her house and she did one last walk-through. I sat on the couch to give her time to do what she needed to do, but really I just wanted to hold her for as long as I could. A few minutes passed and I heard sniffling coming from somewhere, so I walked down the hallway to find Holland sitting on her bed, her face buried in her hands.

"Don't cry," I said as I sat next to her.

She leaned her head against my chest and I wrapped my arms around her, holding her tightly against me. I heard a small laugh escape her lips and she looked up at me, her face damp with tears. As I wiped them away, she leaned into me and kissed me.

"Are you okay?" I asked. "Do you regret last night?"

Holland looked up at me and shook her head, her eyes wide. "Never."

"Me either," I said.

Her parents pulled into the driveway and the time we had both been dreading had finally arrived. All summer, this day had had the ability to threaten our time together, but for the most part, we didn't let it ruin what we had. Now each second felt like it approached faster than the last. I wanted everything to stop so I could tell her all the ways she made me happy, but I was left the only the important parts to share.

"I love you," I whispered to Holland as we stood at her front door.

My forehead was rested against hers, and I was afraid if I looked into her eyes I'd see my own pain reflected there. I knew it was time to say goodbye, but I was not any more ready than I had been three days earlier. We made no promises of making it work, though deep down that was what I wanted.

"I love you too."

"Are you sure you don't want me to go with you?"

"Of course I want you to come with me. But if you do, I might not let you leave me."

"Well, if you don't get into the car now, I might not let you go."

She laughed softly and finally took a step away. When she looked up into my eyes, I could tell she was fighting back the tears. I pulled her into my arms and held her tightly against me, cataloging her scent to memory. Holland's world was about to change, and I didn't want to be the thing holding her back from experiencing all of it. Still, the idea of her moving on without me cut me to the core.

"I don't want this to end," she said.

"We always knew this was going to happen," I reminded her.

"Or we change it."

I kissed her once and smiled. "How?"

"I'll come see you. You come see me. We talk every day…"

"Isn't that what everyone says?"

"We're not everyone. We're special."

"I think we're special too."

"I want you with me."

"Maybe I'll be there in the spring," I told her.

She let out a small gasp and nodded. I hadn't told her where all I planned to apply again, but Westview and Stedham had always been my top choices. Granted, Westview had one thing that the others didn't—it had the girl I loved. We said our goodbyes, and she was able to leave with hope of things working out between us. I stood outside by my car as Mr. Monroe's truck pulled out of the driveway. Holland waved and they started their drive down the street but stopped suddenly.

The back passenger door opened and Holland came running out toward me and jumped into my arms. I held her against me as we kissed once more, but it felt hopeful. This wasn't the end of our story.

It was just the first chapter.

CHAPTER 27

HOLLAND

Four months later

The drive from Westview took nearly five hours due to the holiday traffic. My finals were done and I was looking forward to a nice long break without deadlines and waking up for early morning classes. My roommate ended up being a bit quirky, but we got along well and I imagined we would probably live together beyond freshman year.

Dorm life was a whole new experience—especially living on a coed floor. Our neighbors next door, Dan and Geoff, were insanely funny and always ready to hang out—even if that meant just studying. Milo had visited one weekend, and I had worried that he might feel threatened by the friendship I had forged with Geoff, but the two of them got along really well and that made me so happy.

Distance for Milo and me took a lot of getting used to. After spending nearly every day together during the summer, we were resigned to Facetime calls and texts. It was no substitute for the real thing, but at least we were trying. And we were crushing it. We made sure to talk every morning and he was my last call every night. He was worth waiting for, and though the future was still so uncertain, I did not mind the anticipation to see how it all turned out.

For the first time in months, all five Monroes—plus Harper—would be under one roof. Mom had invited my aunts, uncle, and cousins over for a Christmas party since everyone would be spread all over the place for the holiday. And that meant Milo would be my plus-one.

"I'll be back," I called out to Mom and Dad, who were busy settling Ben and Harper into their room.

"Where are you going?" Marcie asked, but I only answered with a smile. "Tell Milo we said hi."

I gave my sister a hug and started to walk out the door when Mom called out to me to go to the grocery store. I had other plans in mind, but I knew she had a lot on her plate so I agreed to help out.

As I backed out of the driveway I felt my phone vibrate. I stopped the car to see a text from Meg.

Meg: My flight is delayed. I won't be home until after midnight. I don't think I'll make it to your parents.
Me: That's okay. I'll come see you tomorrow.
Meg: Ok. I can't wait.
Me: Me too.

As much as I wanted to see Meg, I was thankful that I would have some uninterrupted time with Milo. We had been able to spend a weekend or two together since I left for Westview, but we had mostly relied on texts and long phone calls. None of those made up for the time we got to actually spend together.

The drive to his house felt like it took an eternity, but I knew that was because I was so excited to see him. My hands were sweaty, my stomach filled with butterflies, and I could feel my heart racing in anticipation of finally getting to spend more than a weekend together.

When I pulled into the Davis' driveway, I grabbed the wrapped box that I had left in the back seat. I stared at the house, the light on in the front room, and hurriedly got out of the car ready to see Milo. But as I walked up to the door, I was greeted by Mr. Davis.

"I thought that was you," he said with a smile as he took the steps down to greet me. "How are you, sweetie?"

"I'm good. How are you?"

He hugged me tightly and looked at me when we parted, his head cocked to the side. "What are you doing here?"

"I came to see Milo."

"He's not here."

"He's not? Is he working?"

"No…I—well, he went looking for you."

"I just got home a couple of hours ago. I wanted to surprise him."

Mr. Davis laughed. "I guess he had the same idea."

I turned and looked back at my car and Milo's dad waved me off. "Go find him. I'm sure I'll be seeing plenty of you while you're home."

I nodded and started to hurry out to my car when I saw the box in my hand. I turned around and ran over to Mr. Davis, who was watching as I headed to my car.

"Forget something?" he asked.

The box contained an ornament that I had made for him that had a picture of Milo's mom on it. I had seen the picture over the summer, and when neither of them were looking I had taken a picture of it with my phone.

"Just a little something," I said, handing the box to him.

"Should I wait or open it now?"

He didn't wait for my response, and I chuckled at his excitement opening the box. I wasn't sure how well he could see it under the dim porch light, but when he stared at it, a smile appearing on his lips, I knew he loved it.

"Thank you, Holland." He smiled. "It's perfect."

"I'm so glad you like it."

He gave me a hug and sighed. "I love it."

"Merry Christmas," I said quietly and he nodded.

"Merry Christmas, Holland. Now, go find Milo."

At that, I took off and went back to my house where I expected to find Milo waiting for me, but his car was nowhere in sight. Maybe his dad had heard him wrong and he had gone somewhere else? Instead of wondering where he was and chasing him around, I decided to contact him.

Me: Hey. Where are you?
Milo: ...

I waited as the dots disappeared, only to reappear again. When his message finally arrived, I was confused why it was so vague.

Milo: Here
Me: Where? I went to your house and your dad said you were coming to find me
Milo: No. I went to our spot

We had spent time at so many places over the summer, but the one that came to mind was the lake. I could have asked him for confirmation, but if I drove the twenty minutes out there, I could surprise him. So that was what I did.

When I pulled into the parking lot, I spotted Milo's car in the distance. It was a chilly December night, and I was thankful for the jacket I was wearing as I climbed out of my car. I walked toward the edge of the lake and looked around for Milo, but didn't see him until I neared his car. He was sitting on the hood, staring out at the moonlit water.

"You didn't text back," he said when he heard me approaching.

He slid off the hood and walked toward me, pulling me into his arms the way he did every time he saw me. The warmth of his body felt like it was there only for me, and I found myself sinking into his embrace. When I looked up at him, his lips pressed against mine and I knew I was home.

"I missed you," I whispered before he placed one last kiss to my lips.

"I missed you more."

He threaded our fingers together and guided me to the spot on his car where he had been sitting. The wind was still lending itself to the motionlessness of the lake in front of us. There were so many nights at school that I would think about the night we had our date at the water, when I knew things would never be the same for me. To be there with him once again was everything I needed.

"I have some news," Milo said as he wrapped an arm over my shoulder to help warm me.

"What's that?"

"You're going to get to see a lot more of me."

I sat up a little straighter and turned to face him. I needed Milo to spell it out for me, because if I was wrong I knew I would be disappointed, so I waited for him to share whatever news it was that he had for me.

"I'm going to Westview in the spring."

"You are?" I gasped before wrapping my arms around him, squeezing him tight. "When did you find out?"

"A few days ago."

"And you're just telling me now?" I asked with a laugh. "You're the worst!"

"I wanted to tell you in person. And there's something else."

"What's that?"

"I applied for the Berman-Shaw Academic Scholarship—that was one of the ones that you found—and I got it."

"Are you serious? That's amazing! I'm so happy for you."

"Well, I wouldn't have known about it if you hadn't found it. So thank you."

"Milo, don't you know I just want you to be happy? You deserve all the good things in this world."

He smiled and kissed the top of my head as I leaned against his chest.

"I know that now," he whispered as he exhaled.

T.K. Rapp

Acknowledgments

I'm so grateful to be able to do what I love and even more grateful to those who help make this is reality. Thank you to my editor Amy Jackson who always comes through for me. I appreciate you more than I can express. Melissa Townsend, thank you for encouraging me to finish when I wasn't sure I had it in me.

To Kimberly Adams, the Goose to my Mav, I love you and I'm so thankful that I met you at the beginning of this journey. I will forever cherish your friendship.

Stacey Lynn, I don't think there are enough words to tell you how much I adore you. You have been my constant and I hope I am as good to you as you are to me. Thank you for being, not only my critique partner, but one of my dearest friends.

Also, a huge thank you to the readers who allow me to give you an escape from reality. Trust me, it's my escape too. And to those people in my life who share my ups and downs: The Tenacious Ten +1, my Wolfpack (Spence, Kim & Kenny), Kari, Bonnie, & Lisa.

Last, but never least, my family. This has been a crazy year and it's only going to be crazier. My daughters and my husband are the most patient and supportive people in my life. They give me time to work when I need it, and remind me to keep going when all I want to do is crash. Thank you for always reminding me that my place is with you.

About the Author

T.K. Rapp is a Texas girl born and raised. She earned a B.A. in Journalism from Texas A&M and it was there that she met the love of her life. He had a contract with the U.S. Navy that would take them across both coasts, and ultimately land them back home in Texas.

Upon finally settling in Texas, T.K. worked as a graphic designer and photographer for the family business that her mom started years earlier. She was able to infuse her creativity and passion, into something she enjoyed, but something was still missing. There was a voice in the back of her head that told her to write, so write, she did. And, somewhere on an external hard drive, are several stories she started and never finished.

Now at home, raising her two daughters, T.K. has more time to do the things she loves, which includes photography and writing. When she's not doing one of those, she can be found with her family, which keeps her busy. She enjoys watching her kids in their various sporting activities (i.e. doing the soccer mom thing), having Sunday breakfast at her parent's house, singing out loud and out of key or dancing like a fool. She loves raunchy humor, gossip blogs and a good book.

Visit T.K. Rapp online:

FACEBOOK
TWITTER
GOODREADS
T.K.RAPP'S WEBSITE
MODEST VIEW BLOG

If you enjoyed this book, check out the others by T.K. Rapp:

Being There
Mine to Lose
Mine to Steal
Fumbled (GOB #1)
Played (GOB #2)
Finding Laila (YA Novel)
The Upside of Regret (YA Novel)
Forgiving Cole

53981011R00137

Made in the USA
Middletown, DE
12 July 2019